fun

An electrifying
page-turner -
perfect for readers
who like their
lightning fa

chapter leaves you on
a cliffhanger, leaving
you in suspense
d more.'

LA, age 9

Hello!

We're back, with another exciting adventure for Holly and her friends! Writing this story was SO much fun, and this time Cathy and I knew exactly how to tell it. There's EVEN MORE artwork in this story than the first, so feast your eyes on the amazingness!

Since ELECTRIGIRL was published, I've been reading loads more comics. If you're into Marvel superheroes, you MUST check out the fantastic MS MARVEL, who is a Muslim girl with superhero powers who still has to deal with her strict parents. I've also laughed all the way through PHOEBE AND HER UNICORN by Dana Simpson, which reminds me of GARFIELD, a comic strip I loved as a kid. But my favourite find is EVIL EMPEROR PENGUIN by Laura Ellen Anderson, which is not only laugh-out-loud funny but also has cracking plots and a hopelessly inept villain.

Happy reading! And watch out for the DEADLY SWARM...!

CHARACTER PROFILES

HOLLY is a perfectly normal 12-year-old who's been struck by weird lighting and can now create and control electricity. Also known as **ELECTRIGIRL**!

JOE is her younger brother, superhero and comics geek and training mentor. Not many superheroes get to be bossed around by their younger brother.

IMOGEN is Holly's best friend since forever. Resourceful and clever, Imogen's favourite hobby is drawing, and she's rarely without her sketchbook.

CAMERON lives in Polperro, where his parents run a caravan park. Cameron loves myths and legends and is obsessed with health and safety.

MAVERICK would like to be James Bond. He does actually work for a shadowy government agency, so he's already got some great gadgets.

PROFFESSOR MACAVITY is a technological genius bent on world domination. Beaten by Holly and her friends in their first encounter, but where is she now…?

FOR MY SUPERHERO MUM
WITH LOVE
J. C.

FOR MY SPARKY NIECE, MOO (BECAUSE SHE'S AMAZING
AND BECAUSE HER SISTER GOT THE LAST DEDICATION AND
I'D NEVER HEAR THE LAST OF IT OTHERWISE!)
#LOVEYOUBOTHEQUALLY xx
C. B.

OXFORD
UNIVERSITY PRESS

Great Clarendon Street, Oxford OX2 6DP
Oxford University Press is a department of the University of Oxford.
It furthers the University's objective of excellence in research, scholarship,
and education by publishing worldwide. Oxford is a registered trade mark
of Oxford University Press in the UK and in certain other countries

Copyright © Jo Cotterill 2016
Illustrations © Cathy Brett 2016

The moral rights of the author have been asserted

Database right Oxford University Press (maker)

First published 2016

British Library Cataloguing in Publication Data

Data available

ISBN: 978-0-19-274592-7

1 3 5 7 9 10 8 6 4 2

Printed in Great Britain

Paper used in the production of this book is a natural,
recyclable product made from wood grown in sustainable forests.
The manufacturing process conforms to the environmental
regulations of the country of origin.

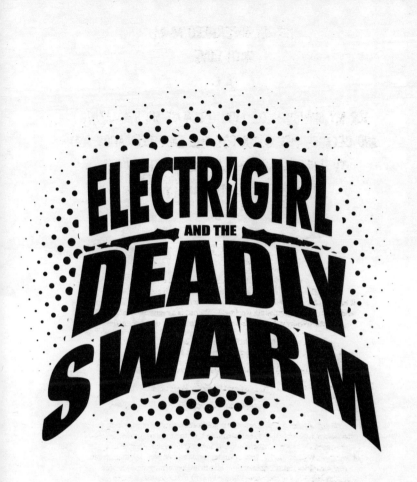

JO COTTERiLL
ILLUSTRATED BY CATHY BRETT

OXFORD
UNIVERSITY PRESS

PREVIOUSLY IN ELECTRIGIRL

PROFESSOR MACAVITY, HEAD OF THE EVIL CYBERSKY CORPORATION, TRIED TO WIPE HER OUT . . .

BUT HOLLY'S BROTHER JOE AND HER BEST FRIEND IMOGEN WERE ON HAND TO SAVE HER.

NOW NO ONE ELSE MUST KNOW HOLLY'S SECRET . . . THAT SHE IS **ELECTRIGIRL**

CHAPTER 1

There should be a law against rain in the summer holidays. School finished two weeks ago, and we've barely had a single day without rain. I hate it when it rains. It means I can't get outside, and I go **BONKERS** when I'm cooped up indoors.

I've never liked being indoors for too long. But since—well—since the whole nearly-dying-in-freaky-world-domination-plot thing at the end of term, I've liked it even less. I try so hard not to think about what happened, but it's not that easy. My brother Joe says, 'Don't show fear. If you show fear, the bad guys have won,' which is typical of him, and all very well if you haven't got superpowers that could destroy the world . . .

I don't mean to make stuff explode! I've done loads of training, but when I get anxious, accidents happen. Mum still doesn't know it was me who short-circuited the TV. Joe was steaming mad because the latest Avengers film was due to be shown that night and we couldn't watch it. He didn't speak to me for a whole eight hours.

I did say sorry a lot.

But today the sun is shining at last! And so I invited my best friend Imogen round, and we went into the garden.

'Blown anything up lately?' Imogen asked, as I bounced on the trampoline. She sounded sympathetic.

I pulled a face (which is not easy to do when you're bouncing). 'I'm trying not to. Joe's given me some more focus exercises to do. I'm training every day.'

Imogen hesitated and then said, 'Do you think maybe you're doing too much?'

'I can't train too much!' I exclaimed. 'She could be *anywhere*, Imogen! She could be watching me right *now*! I have to be ready!'

Imogen didn't ask who 'she' was. We both knew. Professor Macavity, insane technological genius. The one who nearly killed us all only a few weeks ago. 'But there's been no word from her,' Imogen pointed out. 'No sign, since she sent that threatening text.'

'That doesn't mean she's not about to attack,' I said, and felt a shiver pass through me, even in the bright sunshine. I'd ruined her plans, and the professor had vowed to get her revenge. I didn't know when or where it would be, but I knew she'd be back. 'Look,' I said, to take my mind off things, 'look what I've been practising.'

Higher and higher I bounced, feeling electrical charges tingle through my fingers and scalp.

AND THEN I TUNED INTO MY POWERS, FELT THEM START TO FLOW . . .

BOING!

FIZ

FIZZ

FIZZ

WITH NO ONE BUT IMOGEN TO SEE,
HOLLY COULD REALLY LET GO!

I released my powers and felt the electricity flow away, landing back on the trampoline with a bit of a bump. I grinned at Imogen. 'Cool, isn't it?'

'How do you do it?'

I waved a hand at the metal poles that held up the trampoline net. 'These are all metal, so they conduct electricity. Because they go all the way round, I can make a kind of electric net with me inside, and that keeps me off the ground.'

'That's amazing!' Imogen's eyes lit up. 'Do you think you could use it to really fly? Up there?'

I shook my head. 'I need a circle of things that conduct electricity. I don't think birds or clouds would do!'

'It makes your scar glow,' Imogen said.

Self-consciously, I rearranged my fringe to cover my forehead. Thin red wavy lines decorated the smooth skin there, a result of my brush with Macavity and her evil corporation, **⬢CyberSky**. 'I wish it wasn't so obvious. I hate it when people notice.'

'It's not as obvious as you think,' Imogen said, but I could tell she was just saying it to make me feel better.

'Come on in out of the rain,' said Mum, and she smiled at the two of us. 'We're going to have a lovely time.'

I tried to smile at both of them, but inside I was quivering with fear. When would Macavity make her move?

'Hey, you want one of these?' My younger brother came bounding down the garden with a handful of lollies.

'Thanks, Joe.' I took one.

'Not my idea,' he said. 'Mum made me. I'm in the middle of shooting.'

Imogen unwrapped her ice lolly and folded the paper into a neat square. 'What are you filming today?'

'The Hulk versus King Kong,' said Joe enthusiastically. 'I've made an Empire State Building for the final showdown.' My brother is *obsessed* with superheroes. He reads every comic he can get his hands on, and he loves making his own films. I accidentally melted his video camera when I got my powers, but he managed to borrow another one only last week, so he was back to building cardboard sets and designing gadgets for his supervillains.

Imogen raised her eyebrows. 'Who wins?'

Joe was scandalized. 'I can't tell you that. You'll have to watch the film when it's finished.'

'You might not want to be around for that,' I suggested to Imogen with a grin.

Joe made an indignant snort. 'Yeah, keep laughing. You won't be laughing when I get my Oscar for Best Director.'

'Are you going to film when you're down in Cornwall?' asked Imogen.

Joe's eyes lit up. 'I hadn't thought of that. Yeah—I could use the rock pools, or the sand. Sand lairs!'

I groaned. 'Oh, thanks, Imogen. Looks like I'm going to be playing on my own this holiday.'

'I wish I was coming,' she said quietly.

I felt bad. 'I wish you were, too; it's so much fun down there. Such a pain your dad can't get the time off. Dads should get way more holiday time. If my dad weren't in some random country doing something army-ish, he could come with us. And if you came I could show you all the cool beaches and stuff. There's rock pools and swimming and climbing and all sorts.'

Imogen smiled a bit. 'It's more likely I'd want to sit and draw all day.'

I shrugged. 'I wouldn't mind. You could

draw in the morning and swim with me in the afternoon. Your parents don't even need to come! My mum would look after us.' I knew, even as I said it, that it was no good. Imogen's mum had already said no—twelve times.

Imogen sighed. 'Sorry. Mum's paranoid. She thinks I'm going to be kidnapped all over again.'

I bit my lip. Being friends with me made Imogen a possible target for Professor Macavity. I hated it, but it was true.

'If you were,' Joe said through a mouthful of wafer, 'we could get the government to sort it.'

I rolled my eyes. 'It's not the government. It's just Steve.'

'*Secret* government,' he said darkly. 'Shadowy undercover department . . .'

'They're keeping an eye on *her*, you know,' Imogen said to me reassuringly. 'Steve said they were. If she was coming after you, we'd know.'

'It's not just about me, though, is it?' I said. 'She knows you're my friend. Joe's my brother. Just by being with me, you're putting yourselves in danger.'

'That's the job,' Joe said, shrugging. 'I can't just un-brother you, can I? Plus, I'm your mentor.' He puffed out his chest in pride. I'd agreed to let Joe be my superhero mentor since he read more comics than anyone I knew, but sometimes he took his job way too seriously.

Imogen looked less confident. 'I still have dreams about her.'

I shivered again. 'Me too.' Almost instinctively, I felt in my pocket for the pager Steve had given me. I took it everywhere—even into the bathroom. He'd said if there were the slightest hint we were in danger, he'd be in touch. But the pager had stayed silent for weeks now.

'Look,' said Joe, echoing my thoughts, 'there's nothing to worry about. If there was an emergency, we'd be told.'

'Kids!' Mum was standing at the back door calling. 'Kids, can you come up here a minute? We've got an emergency!'

CHAPTER 2

Imogen's mum had come to pick her up. She looked worried. 'Sorry, love,' she said to Imogen. 'Something's happened.'

I felt sick. This was it. Macavity had found us—and now Imogen would pay for being my best friend. I gripped the door frame for support.

Imogen had gone pale. 'What is it?'

'Your gran's sick,' her mum told her. 'Got a nasty bout of pneumonia. Grandad just rang— they've taken her into hospital.'

For a moment I was bewildered. What did Imogen's gran's pneumonia have to do with Macavity?!

'Oh,' said Imogen, and I wondered whether she too was baffled. 'Is she . . . is she going to . . .'

Her mum shook her head quickly. 'Oh, no! No, we hope not. The hospital is looking after her—but your grandad isn't in the best of health either, and we need to go up there.'

'Up?' I asked. 'Up where?'

'Scotland,' Imogen said. 'They live in Scotland.' She didn't sound pleased. 'I thought Dad couldn't get time off.'

'Your dad won't come. Just you and me.' Her mum tried to smile. 'It'll be a mum and daughter road trip.'

'How long for?'

'Not sure. Maybe two or three weeks.'

'What?!' Imogen looked horrified. 'But there's nothing to do up there! They live in the middle of nowhere!'

'I can't help that,' her mum said. 'We'll take some puzzles. And your sketchbooks.'

Imogen gazed at me, helpless. I felt sorry for her. I mean, it was awful that her gran was sick, but being stuck in the middle of nowhere for three weeks didn't sound like much fun to me.

Mum coughed. 'Er . . . well, Imogen could always come to Cornwall with us.'

I let out a kind of **SQUEAK** and stuffed my fist into my mouth.

Then there was a **LOT** of talking—by my mum and Imogen's mum and Imogen. And I said NOTHING AT ALL but I made my eyes as pleading and big as they could possibly go.

And finally Imogen's mum said she could come with us, and I just went 'YES!!' and did an air punch, and then Imogen and I did loads of hugging and jumping up and down until her mum reminded us that her gran was really sick and that this wasn't something to be happy about. And so we tried to calm down, and Imogen and her mum went home.

Mum smiled at me. 'Things have a way of working out, don't they? And the caravan sleeps four, so it's going to be fine.'

'Yes, but one is a double bed.' Joe looked suddenly appalled. 'I won't have to *share* with someone, will I?!'

Mum laughed. 'No, Holly and Imogen can share. Or I can share with Holly.'

'I'll share with Imogen,' I said immediately. 'No offence, Mum, but you snore.'

Her jaw dropped. 'I do not!'

'You **SO** do,' Joe and I said at the same time.

My best friend was coming with us on holiday! I was thrilled—and also terrified. Because if Imogen came to Cornwall with us, would I be putting her in danger again?

Mind you, if Professor Macavity wanted to kidnap Imogen, it wouldn't matter whether she was in Scotland or Cornwall or Timbuktu. Maybe it was better to have Imogen close by, so I could protect her with my powers. But what if Macavity turned up and I couldn't stop her?

'You're panicking about nothing,' Joe told me, when I confessed my fears to him later. He tapped the pager that I was gripping. 'This isn't going off, is it?'

I peered at it. 'Maybe the battery's dead. Maybe it's not working!'

'Stop it,' Joe said. 'Even superheroes need a holiday. Can you imagine Professor Macavity on a beach?'

That terrifying, grey-suited, grey-haired, grey-eyed, sharp-faced woman . . . on a beach? No, I couldn't imagine it. The very idea made me laugh.

'See?' said Joe. 'Stop worrying. It's going to be **AWESOME**!'

CHAPTER 3

It rained **ALL THE WAY** to Cornwall. 'It's going to be **AWFUL**,' I muttered for about the tenth time.

Mum did that thing where she presses her lips together really hard to stop herself saying something rude. There are no straight roads on the south coast, and we had to stop three times because Imogen was feeling sick. 'Sorry,' she said. 'I usually take tablets but I forgot.' After she really *was* sick, Mum let her sit in the front.

Joe was glued to his DVD player, watching back-to-back Spider-Man films. I watched a bit of something but then got fidgety. It's a VERY LONG WAY to Polcarrow, which is nearly off the end of the country. And being cooped up was really getting to me, which was NOT good for my electricity issues.

By the time we finally pulled into the gravel

driveway of the caravan park, I was ready to burst—and had given myself three static shocks from the metal buckle on my seat belt.

'It's raining here, too,' said Imogen in dismay as we got out of the car.

I was so relieved to be out in the open space again. But the weather was DISMAL. The sea, only half a mile away, was shrouded in grey mist. I felt bad that I'd bigged up the place to my friend, only for it to be so disappointing when we arrived. 'The view is amazing when it's not like this.'

'Come on,' said Mum. 'Let's find our caravan and have a nice cup of tea.'

'Hello!'

A tall boy with scrubby black hair and rain-spattered glasses was heading towards us. 'I'm Cameron,' he said, staring at us one at a time. 'Welcome to Polcarrow.'

'Thank you,' said my mum, smiling.

Cameron didn't smile back. 'My parents run the caravan park. Have you booked with us?'

'Yes,' said Mum. 'The name's Sparkes.'

'One adult and two children, aged twelve and ten, Holly and Joseph,' Cameron said immediately, his gaze flicking between me and Joe and Imogen. It was a bit weird—I mean, did he have a photographic memory or something? Did he know the names of *every* person arriving today?

'Yes,' said Mum. 'We've got an extra.' She turned to smile at Imogen.

'She's not on the list,' Cameron said.

'She could only come at the last minute,' I explained. 'Her mum had to go to Scotland to look after her gran because she's ill.'

Cameron turned his big brown eyes on me. 'The mother's ill?' he said. 'Or the grandmother?'

I stared at him. Was he an idiot? 'The grandmother, of course.'

His brow creased as his gaze slid to my forehead. 'What's that on your head? Have you got a skin condition?'

Instinctively, I reached up to pull my fringe across to hide my scar. 'It's nothing.'

'Is it psoriasis?' he asked. 'I know someone with psoriasis.'

'I don't even know what that is,' I snapped.

'Is your mother around?' Mum interrupted. 'I could do with talking to her about bringing Imogen.'

'We have to have all the names for fire

regulations,' Cameron told her. 'It's the rules.'

I could feel my powers rising along with my temper. Honestly, Cameron was so annoying! And so rude! Asking me about my scar right out like that!

Thankfully, just at that moment, a woman came into view. She had the same wild hair as Cameron and the same brown eyes, but hers were more friendly. 'Hello!' she said. 'Sorry about the weather; what bad luck for your arrival day! Don't stand in the drizzle though—come in while we get you sorted.'

Glaring at Cameron, I followed Mum and the others into a Portakabin on the edge of the car park.

'I'm Julie,' said the woman, 'and you've already met my son Cameron.'

Cameron was waiting patiently outside the cabin, seemingly unbothered by the rain. 'He said Imogen couldn't stay with us because she wasn't on the list,' I said.

Julie smiled. 'He's very hot on the rules, my Cam. Doesn't like last-minute changes. He's always been like that, since he was little.' She laughed. 'I never have to worry that he'll do something dangerous. He'll probably grow up to be a health and safety officer. Now, then, where's my file?' She reached up to the little shelf and took down a thick black folder. 'Here we are . . . Sparkes. That's fine. Your caravan has plenty of room for a fourth person. I'll just add her name to the list.'

I breathed a sigh of relief, and within minutes we were trooping back outside with the key for caravan number seventeen.

'I'll show you the way,' Cameron said, in an almost friendly tone of voice. He even gave a kind of smile. I glared back at him.

'I hope he doesn't hang around all the time,' I whispered to Imogen as we tramped along the gravel path. 'He's really annoying.'

'He does seem kind of bossy,' she agreed.

Joe came up behind me. 'You could zap him,' he whispered mischievously.

I was seriously tempted.

'No,' said Imogen. 'You mustn't use your powers on people. It's not fair.'

I raised my eyebrows pointedly.

'Er . . . unless they're evil, of course,' she added. 'And planning to take over the world. And I don't think Cameron fits into that category.'

'He might,' I said darkly. 'We don't know

yet.' A sudden fear gripped me. Was Cameron *normal*? Only a few weeks ago, I'd seen people I knew turn into near-zombies thanks to CyberSky's creepy evil mobile phones. What if ... what if Cameron was under the control of Professor Macavity? What if she was actually here, already, waiting for me—and Cameron was part of her trap?!

My feet slowed on the path, and I looked around fearfully.

Imogen glanced back. 'Come on, Holly! I can't wait to see our caravan!'

I made an effort to smile. 'Yeah.'

'Here we are,' said Cameron, as we reached number seventeen. 'You should find everything you need inside. There's a shop down the road for milk and bread and things. I hope you've brought torches because it's not safe to wander around at night time, and we don't want anyone to fall into the sea. Stay away from the cliff edge. Remember to switch the gas stove off when you've finished using it.'

'I know how to use a stove,' Mum said, with an edge to her voice.

He turned his brown eyes on her. 'Some

people blew up their caravan once,' he said. 'They left the gas on and then lit a match. *Boom*.'

There was a pause.

A cold fear settled in my stomach. Was he warning me? Was this what Macavity was planning? To blow us up in our own caravan?

'Right,' said Mum brightly. 'Thanks so much, Cameron, I'll take it from here.'

'There are guidebooks on the side . . .' Cameron began.

'Good*bye*,' said Mum firmly, opening the door and beckoning us in.

'Oh. Goodbye.' Cameron gave a shrug and headed off. I stepped back jerkily as he passed, banging my arm on the caravan door. Was he going to report to Macavity right now?

'I AM NOT A TOASTER!' I yelled, throwing off the covers and sitting bolt upright. Then I realized where I was. Early-morning light streamed in through the thin caravan curtains. 'Oh! Um . . .'

Imogen was staring at me in fright from the other side of the bed. 'Holly? What's the matter? Are you all right?'

'What's going on?' Mum appeared in the doorway, a hand clutching the side of her head. 'Holly? Is everything OK?'

From the other end of the caravan, I could hear Joe muttering, 'Bad dreams.'

'Oh, Holly,' Mum said, coming to give me a hug. 'I'm sorry. Were you dreaming about your accident again?'

'Yes,' I said, hugging her back. I didn't like lying to Mum, but she didn't know the truth about me or about what really happened in Macavity's underground HQ. She believed I'd got the scar on my head from a gas explosion in the building.

Imogen rubbed her face. 'You gave me a fright. I thought the kitchen was blowing up, like Cameron warned us.'

Mum snorted. 'I know how to operate a stove, thank you very much. Why don't the three of you go out for a walk while I get breakfast? You could show Imogen the cove.' She pulled open the curtain. 'Look, the sun's out.'

'It's not raining?' Suddenly, I couldn't bear to be inside for a minute longer. 'Come on, let's go!'

Mum laughed. 'Maybe you should get dressed first.'

Joe grumbled but within a few minutes all three of us were outside and walking down to the beach. The caravans were set out in rows, and there were eight more rows before the wide expanse of grass that stretched out between the park and the place where the ground started to slope down to the beach. There was a brisk breeze blowing the trees enthusiastically, and out on the sea I could see little white caps to the waves. Instantly, I felt better. I was Electrigirl! If Macavity *had* sent Cameron after me—well, he'd be no match for me!

'What were you really dreaming about?' asked Imogen.

I told her—including the bit at the end about Cameron and the toast. She giggled. 'Why on earth was *he* in the dream?'

Hesitantly, I admitted, 'Don't you think that

maybe . . . I mean, I know it's crazy . . . but what if he's working for the professor?'

Imogen and Joe both stopped dead and stared at me. 'Holly, have you gone completely insane?'

'She could be here!' I insisted. 'She said she would come after me—where's better than while we're on holiday? Off our guard?'

'Holly,' said Joe patiently, 'you're talking rubbish. Cameron is just a bit weird. He's not an evil sidekick.'

'How do you know?' I challenged him.

He just raised his eyebrows at me.

I deflated. 'I know, I know. It's crazy. I just . . . I see her everywhere. I keep wondering when she's going to come after me.'

'Oh, Holly.' Imogen gave me a hug. 'We'll have warning. Steve will let us know if she's anywhere near us. You've got your pager with you, haven't you?'

I patted my pocket.

'There you are, then. Stop worrying. You can't go around suspecting everyone of being evil, you know.'

I smiled. 'I suppose not. I'm so glad you came with us.'

She grinned back. 'Me too. If only to stop

you going bonkers and blowing us all up. And Cameron wouldn't like that *at all!*'

I laughed. 'I've got to do something, though. I feel all tingly and static after that dream. Is anyone around?'

Joe looked back towards the rows of caravans. 'They're too close. Anyone could be watching. Wait till we're into the dunes.'

The ground dropped away as we approached the beach, the sea sparkling like it was covered in turquoise sequins. There was no one else in sight, and as soon as the caravan park was hidden behind us, Joe said, 'All right, here should be safe. But nothing too big.'

'I promise,' I said.

THEN I CLOSED MY EYES . . .

'Nothing too big?!' my brother groaned, as Cameron came clambering up from the beach to meet us. 'Now you've done it!'

Cameron's eyes were wide. 'Did you SEE that?' he said. 'Where did it come from?'

Typical! It WOULD be him!

'Er . . .' I said, pulling the neckline of my top up to hide any last traces of my burn pattern as it faded. 'Er . . . see what?'

'That light!' said Cameron, turning to look out to sea. He peered into the distance for a moment. 'It's gone now. It was—I don't know *what* it was.'

'I didn't see anything,' Joe jumped in, shooting me a look. 'Just the sun on the sea. It's bright today.'

Cameron shook his head. 'It wasn't that. This was much brighter. Like a shooting star.'

Bother! 'You must have imagined it,' I said, irritated.

He looked offended. 'I don't imagine things. I suppose it might be a discharge from the build-up of electricity in the rocks. I read that can happen when you've got trace metals running through the granite—and the tin mine's not far away. I'd better mention it to Dad later in case he needs to go down and check the safety levels.'

'In the tin mine?' asked Joe, distracted from glaring at me. 'I thought that was all abandoned and locked up. It was last time we were here.'

'It was opened six months ago,' Cameron said. 'My dad takes tour parties down there. It's a really interesting place.'

'Is there still tin down there, then?' Joe's eyes lit up. It was just the kind of thing that got him excited. I did a pretend yawn, but he didn't notice.

Cameron turned to Joe. 'Loads. And copper and iron. They chipped out as much as they could, but it was all by hand. I'll take you down there and show you, if you like. But you have to stick with me. Don't go wandering off down the tunnels on your own.'

'Why not?' I retorted. 'Will the Cornish piskies get us?'

Cameron's dark eyes fixed on me. 'They might.'

I laughed. 'There's no such thing.'

'Yes there is,' he said simply. 'I've seen them.'

I was speechless. The boy was completely off his rocker!

Joe took a step towards him. 'You've *seen* them?' he asked.

'I don't tell lies,' Cameron said. 'Ask my mum. Ask anyone.'

Imogen, Joe and I looked at each other. 'Can *we* see them?' asked Joe.

Cameron hesitated. 'I don't know if I can trust you,' he said.

I was insulted! Him, trust *us*?!

Imogen stepped forward. 'Look,' she said. 'I think we got off on the wrong foot.'

Cameron glanced down at her feet. 'Which one is the wrong one?'

'No,' said Imogen patiently, as I snorted, 'I mean we didn't start off very friendly.' She smiled and held out her hand. 'I'm Imogen.'

'Oh,' said Cameron, and then to my astonishment his face broke into a smile. He shook her hand. 'Hello. I'm Cameron.'

'Go on.' Imogen nudged Joe, who also stepped forward to shake hands and introduce himself.

Then Cameron turned to me, holding out his hand. Behind his back, I could see Imogen urgently mouthing, '*Be nice!*' at me.

'Oh, all *right*!' I said. 'Hi, I'm Holly.' I shook

his hand. It felt dry and cool.

Cameron beamed at me. It was quite bizarre to see him smiling. 'It's very nice to meet you all. I don't have many friends in Polcarrow.'

I wanted to say, 'Really? Can't imagine why,' but stopped myself.

'I thought piskies were just a myth,' Imogen said. 'Like fairies.'

'Oh, no.' Cameron was insistent. 'They're real. I've seen them. In fact . . .' his voice dropped and he looked around to see if anyone was within earshot, 'I'll show you, if you like. I've got one in a jar.'

CHAPTER 5

'He *can't* be telling the truth,' I muttered to Joe, as we followed Cameron down the path to the beach. We'd been back to the caravan for breakfast, and Mum had sent us off again so that she could go to the shop to stock up. I made sure my pager was in my shorts pocket, as always, and Joe was carrying his old mobile phone, in case Mum needed to call. 'Piskies aren't real. They're just not.'

'Sherlock Holmes said that when you've eliminated the impossible, whatever remains, even if it seems completely mad, must be the truth,' Joe muttered back.

Cameron glanced back at us, grinning. 'Keep up!'

'I still don't trust him,' I said mutinously.

Joe sighed. 'Look, he's not Macavity in a mask, is he?' He ran on to catch up with the others, while I panicked about what he'd just said. *What if Cameron was Macavity in a mask?*

No, he couldn't be. The professor wore grey, all over—and even if she were dressed differently and wore a wig, her voice would still be the same. I'd know that lifeless monotone anywhere—the very memory of it sent chills down my spine.

Mind you, the thought *did* bring me comfort. Wherever Macavity was, she couldn't disguise herself from me. I'd always know her, as soon as she spoke. I ran to catch up with the others.

'Ooh!' squeaked Imogen as we reached the edge of the sand. 'Shells!'

'Not now,' I said, grinning. 'We didn't bring a bucket, and we're going to see a piskie.'

'But . . .' Imogen came reluctantly, looking longingly at the piles of shells at the high tide line.

'I'll show you where the best ones are later,' offered Cameron. 'Just as long as you don't go over the rocks. It's not safe.'

Imogen and I grinned at each other. Cameron really was the king of health and safety!

It was still early, so the beach wasn't full of holidaymakers yet. A few families were trudging along, weighed down by bags and arguing about where to set up camp for the day. I took off my sandals and wriggled my toes in the sand. That felt better!

Cameron led us along the beach to the right, where the land rose sharply and grey rocks jutted out onto the sand. Here and there, shadows darkened the rocks. My heart beat faster. I wasn't a fan of darkness and enclosed spaces . . .

Cameron didn't hesitate. He ducked into a dark opening at the base of the cliff. Imogen and Joe followed. I took a breath. Calm, Holly. Focus. Just breathe.

'You coming?' It was Joe's voice.

I took another deep breath and followed them in, moving slowly while my eyes adjusted to the sudden darkness. Cameron had a torch, but the thin beam played over the rocks ahead, leaving me to edge my feet forward on unseen ground. The walls were damp and close, and I couldn't help remembering the grey walls of CyberSky . . . the lift that took me and Joe deep underground . . . the clouds of smoke that choked us on our escape, and how I nearly didn't make it out at all . . .

By the time we got to the back of the cave, I was a terrified mess, ready to bolt at any moment. Worse, the beam from Cameron's torch suddenly disappeared—had the batteries gone? 'Hey, what happened to the light?' I heard Joe exclaim. In the dark, in a state of panic, the high levels of adrenalin made my fingers tingle with electricity.

Keep calm, I told myself. Focus. Breathe. Remember your training.

Then something suddenly rushed towards me in the darkness. 'BOO!'

I screamed. 'Get away! Get away!' I raised my hands, ready to strike.

'It's just me!' said Cameron. 'Er—it's me, see?' He switched on the torch and pointed it up at his face.

'You *idiot*!' I told him forcefully. 'I could have killed you!' I wasn't exaggerating, either.

He looked taken aback. 'Sorry. I thought it was funny.'

'Well, it *wasn't*,' I snarled.

'I can show you the piskie now,' he said hurriedly. 'To make up for it. Here.' He turned his torch onto the wall. At first I couldn't see anything, but he reached out an arm, and I realized that there was a kind of shelf, a place where the rock hollowed itself out into a natural cupboard. There was a scraping noise, and Cameron pulled out a large glass jar, like the ones you get pickled eggs in at fish and chip shops. A sudden skittering noise from inside the jar made us all jump, and I felt Imogen's hand clutch at my arm.

'What the . . .' whispered Joe. 'What *is* it?'

Cameron held up the jar, and then pointed the torch so that its beam fell squarely onto what was inside.

I forgot to breathe.

Inside the jar was something small—something about the length of my finger. It was hard to make out, but in shape it looked like a daddy long-legs: thin and spidery, with a pair of wings that fluttered in vain against the sides of the jar.

And it had eyes. Two tiny green eyes that glowed brightly in the light of the torch.

'I don't believe it,' Joe whispered.

'A piskie,' said Imogen softly. 'A real piskie.'

'But it can't be . . .' I said. I couldn't take my eyes off it. The tiny thing skittered and flapped inside its glass prison.

'It is,' Cameron said proudly. 'It's my piskie and I found it, and I'm keeping it safe. See? I told you they were real.'

CHAPTER 6

'You shouldn't keep it in there,' Imogen said. 'It's trying to get out—can't you see?'

Joe was still peering at the jar, his nose only centimetres away. The piskie's wings flashed in the torch beam. 'If only it would stay still so I could get a proper look,' he murmured. 'We need to get it out into the light so I can see it better.'

'No!' Cameron cradled the jar in his arms. 'You can't! If anyone else knows, they'll want to dissect it!'

I stared at the frantic thing. I had some sympathy. I couldn't tell anyone my secret either, for fear of being experimented on by people who wanted my powers.

'It could be just a really big insect,' Joe said, still squinting.

Cameron glared at him. 'It's a piskie. Trust me. And there are more. Loads more. Not here—

somewhere else. They're hiding from humans—wouldn't *you*, if you were a piskie? I was lucky to trap one without waking the others.'

'Can I hold it?' Imogen stretched out her hands.

'No!' Cameron stepped back, jerking the jar out of her reach. But his actions were clumsy and as he swung back his arm, the jar bashed into the shelf of rock behind him.

There was the sound of shattering glass, and the torch beam wobbled wildly across the cave ceiling and then fell to the floor, plunging us all into darkness once more. My breath stopped in my throat and my hands clenched convulsively. I froze to the spot. Cameron let out a shout of horror. 'You idiot! It's broken!'

Something flitted past my face in the darkness, and I closed my eyes, feeling my heart pound as the panic gripped me. I needed to find the exit! We had to get out! Before the building collapsed on top of us and we were trapped down here in the smoke with Macavity! My brain tried to tell me—*you're in a cave, not CyberSky*—but it was no good. My powers were springing to the surface!

Instantly, I felt my powers recede. The darkness was still frightening, but now my head felt a bit clearer. I didn't actually mean to zap the piskie like that—but it had a stinger! What kind of piskie has a stinger?!

Cameron dived for the creature on the floor. 'What did you DO?' he cried. 'You've killed it!'

'I'm sorry.' I took a step forward, but he gathered the tiny thing up in his hands, tucking the torch under his arm.

'It's mine! Get away from me! *You're dangerous!*'

I blinked back sudden tears. No matter how much training I did, somehow I always made a mess of things! It wasn't long ago that I blew up my classroom.

Joe touched me on the arm. 'We need to have a talk,' he said quietly. 'Mentor stuff.'

I nodded and wiped my eyes. Although it was kind of annoying to be told what to do by my younger brother, he *did* know more about this kind of thing than I did.

There was no point keeping the piskie hidden in the cave now. We trooped back to the beach, Imogen reaching for my hand on the way to give it a squeeze. I felt grateful she was sympathetic. My hands were shaking, and I was very relieved to be outside again.

Cameron sat down on the sand, just outside the cave. There was a mark on his lower arm that looked like a bee sting. The piskie's wings and legs hung limply from his clasped hands. He dropped the torch and opened his hands very slowly. 'It's not moving. I think it's dead.' He sounded devastated.

'I'm so sorry,' I said, feeling utterly rubbish. 'I didn't mean to, but it was heading right for me.'

Joe crouched next to Cameron. 'Can you put it down? So we can see it properly?'

Cameron reluctantly laid the creature down on the sand. In the sunlight, it seemed strangely grey and spindly, arms and legs glinting slightly, and the wings revealing a kind of pattern that . . . looked kind of familiar.

Joe peered at it, his face set in concentration. 'I don't understand . . .' he said. 'This isn't . . . I mean . . . it isn't . . .'

Imogen said in a puzzled voice, 'Is that . . . *metal*?'

I leaned over to see. 'What? Where?'

'Everywhere. All over.' Joe sat back. 'The

whole thing is made of tiny metal parts, even the wings.

THIS ISN'T AN INSECT.
IT'S A ROBOT.'

'A robot? But . . .' I stared down at it. I'd never seen a robot like that before. It looked like a fairy—well, if fairies were about eight centimetres tall, and made of shiny grey metal. It had two arms and two legs, and a pair of really magnificent wings, with a criss-crossing pattern that made me frown. Why did it remind me of something?

'It's *awesome!*' Joe said, with force. 'I mean, it's like a drone. Those planes or helicopters you can operate with remote control . . . they're brilliant—but *this!*' He shook his head. 'I'd sell my sister for one of these.'

'Thanks very much!' I said, offended.

'So it . . . it wasn't *alive?*' asked Imogen. 'It's not a real piskie?'

Joe glanced at Cameron, who seemed to be stunned. 'No, sorry. It must run on batteries.'

'It's not a piskie?' whispered Cameron. He was staring at the robot on the sand as though he couldn't believe what he was seeing.

'It's way cooler than a piskie,' Joe said, trying to be reassuring. 'I mean, this is a really amazing design. See this?' He pointed at a tiny metal arm, which ended in a sharp spike rather than a hand. 'That's how it stung you. Piskies don't carry spikes, do they?'

Cameron rubbed the mark on his arm. 'I didn't want it dead,' he said. Then he turned to glare up at me. 'You shouldn't have done that.'

'I'm sorry.'

'What *was* that anyway?' He got to his feet. 'There was all this light round you, and then something like *lightning* came out of your *hand* . . .'

I took a breath. What could I say? I glanced at Joe and Imogen, who stared back at me helplessly. 'You can't tell anyone,' I said to Cameron, and I heard my brother groan. 'What?' I said. 'He saw me! How do I explain it?'

'You have to tell him the truth,' Imogen said. 'It's only fair.'

Joe threw up his hands. 'So much for secrecy!'

I didn't want to tell Cameron. He was the *last*

person I wanted in on my secret, but I owed him an explanation—and what could I say apart from the truth? 'I have this thing I can do,' I said awkwardly. 'A kind of—well, a kind of power. Like, um . . .' This was so embarrassing! It sounded so stupid and impossible out loud! 'I can . . . make electricity.'

He stared at me. 'People lie to me sometimes,' he said, 'and I can't always tell when they do. Or if they're making fun of me.'

'I'm not making fun of you,' I said. 'And I'm not lying. Honestly. I got struck by lightning— and now I can do stuff with electricity. That shooting star you saw this morning on the beach? That was me. Er. Sorry.'

His jaw dropped. 'But that's impossible.'

I grinned. 'Hey, just a minute ago you believed in piskies. Why not a superhero?'

'But you're just a . . . girl.' He blinked. 'You look normal.'

'That's because I am. Mostly.'

Joe broke in. 'Cameron, can I borrow your robot for a bit? I'm dying to look at it under a microscope.'

Cameron turned round. 'No! It's mine! I found it.' He rubbed a hand over his eyes, and for a moment he seemed to stumble.

'Are you okay?' asked Imogen.

'I feel weird,' he said. He bent down to gather up the robot piskie. 'I'm going home for a bit.'

'I could look after the robot for you and bring it over later,' Joe said, pleadingly.

'No!' Cameron suddenly blazed. 'It's mine! Stay away!'

We all stepped back in shock, and Cameron started off back up the beach, his feet making deep impressions in the sand as he stamped. To my surprise, he cut left way before the regular path and began to climb.

'He's going over the rocks!' Imogen said in alarm. 'Why's he doing that?'

Joe stared. 'He told us they were really dangerous.'

'And he's always on about safety,' I added. 'Should we go after him?'

'He doesn't want to have company,' said Imogen. We watched as he climbed higher and higher and had soon disappeared from view.

Joe was frowning. 'What's going on? His mum said he never does anything dangerous!'

'He's upset,' said Imogen. 'He doesn't have many friends, and look what happened when he showed us his treasure.' She glanced at me.

'I didn't mean to!' I said hotly. 'I *told* you! It was an accident! What was I supposed to do? It stung him and then it was coming straight for me!'

'It was precious to him,' Imogen said.

'Oh yeah? He captured what he thought was a *fairy*, and he put it in a glass jar at the back of a *cave*!' I pointed out. 'Did you see any air holes in that jar? Cos I didn't! If it *had* been alive, he'd have killed it anyway!'

'*Holly* . . .'

'What?!' I turned to my brother, wanting him to be on my side. 'This isn't all my fault!'

Joe raised his eyebrows. 'You lost control. You were already running high on energy when we went into the cave.'

'I don't like confined spaces,' I muttered.

'But you've got to stay in control,' Joe said. 'You've got to stop letting your imagination get the better of you.'

'I don't have any imagination,' I snapped. 'People are always telling me that. And it's not imagination to think that someone's after you—because they are! She is! And don't tell me that I'm crazy to see her everywhere! Even that robot is grey, did you notice? Grey, like everything at CyberSky! OH!'

I felt my knees buckle under me. 'Of *course*! *That's* what it was—*that's* where I've seen it!'

'What? Where?' Imogen was staring at me. 'What are you talking about?'

'Its wings!' I said triumphantly. 'The piskie's wings! They've got the same pattern on them as the CyberSky logo!'

There was a pause.

Then Imogen said, 'I really think you're taking this too far, Holly. We're meant to be on holiday.'

My mouth dried. 'You didn't see it?'

'I'm going back to the caravan to get a bucket,' she said. 'And then I'm coming here to collect shells. I don't want to talk about CyberSky. I want a *holiday*.' She turned and stomped off, heading for the path into the dunes further down the beach.

I turned to my brother, imploring. 'Joe, you're my mentor. Didn't you see the pattern on its wings? Didn't it remind you of CyberSky?'

He sighed. 'No, Holly. It didn't.'

I couldn't believe it. How could they not have recognized it? 'You need another look,' I told him. 'If you just look—'

'Well, I can't, can I?' snapped Joe. 'Cameron's got it. So just drop it, all right? I'm going for a walk.'

I stood on the beach as everyone walked away from me. Was I going mad? But surely . . . those wings . . . ! I could prove it to Joe, I knew I could! If he could just see the piskie . . .

Before I knew it, I was heading off up the beach, towards the caravan park, to find Cameron.

CHAPTER 8

I went straight to the owners' cabin by the entrance to the park. Julie was in there, doing some paperwork. She smiled at me. 'Hello, Holly. I had a nice chat with your mum a bit earlier. Now, what can I do for you?'

'Er, I was looking for Cameron,' I said.

'He's not here, love. He might have gone up to the house. You could go and have a look there. Do you know which one it is?'

I shook my head.

'You go left out of the caravan park, and it's the first one you come to,' she told me. 'In a row of four houses. It's before you get to the shop. But maybe you'd better just mention it to your mum before you go? She was telling me you've been through quite an ordeal lately.' Her eyes flicked to the burn pattern on my forehead. 'Don't want her to worry.'

'Oh, I'll only be a minute,' I said, pulling my fringe forward. Before she could say anything else, I was out of the cabin and running down the driveway to the main road.

Their house was easy to spot. It was a normal-looking grey-brick house, with a black front door and big windows at the front and a chimney and . . .

I stopped dead in my tracks and gasped.

Cameron was on the roof.

On the roof.

What the . . . what was he doing on the *roof*?!

For a moment, I couldn't think, I was so stunned. Cameron was *obsessed* with safety. His mum had told us he never did anything dangerous and usually told other people off for doing dangerous things—and yet here he was, on his *roof*!

Had he gone crazy? First crossing over the rocks, now this . . . it was almost like he'd suddenly forgotten who he was. I looked up, rooted to the spot in uncertainty. Cameron must have climbed out of one of the top windows. He was making his way along the ridge, one foot either side, slipping and sliding on the slates. When he reached the chimney, he stopped for a moment and reached out.

There was a big TV aerial on the roof. Cameron had hold of the wire and was twisting it, trying to bend it into a new position.

Was he completely and utterly *insane*? One slip . . . one wrong move . . . and he'd be plunging to the ground!

What should I do? I didn't want to shout up to him, in case I startled him and made him fall. Should I run back to his mum and—what? Ask her to call the police? What would they do? Should I stay here, in case he fell off and I was the only witness to what had happened and needed to call an ambulance or something?! Panic gripped me, slowing my brain to a standstill and turning any decision-making to mush.

Cameron seemed to be having difficulty with the aerial. He pushed it and pulled it, and then stepped back to see if it would hold its new position.

And then he slipped.

It was as though I saw it in slow motion. Seriously—like that bullet-time thing they do in films, where the person is suspended in mid-air while the camera goes round them. Or like cartoons, where the rabbit or the wolf runs off the edge of a cliff, realizes they're running on nothing, looks down, looks straight at the camera—and *then* plummets to the ground.

Cameron's right foot slipped on the slate. He flung out an arm to grab hold of the aerial, but he was already tipping too far over and there was no way he could reach it. He slid down the roof, his arms whirling like a windmill, no way of stopping.

WITHOUT EVEN PLANNING IT, HOLLY'S POWERS SWITCHED ON ...

I rushed over, trembling. 'Are you all right?'

Cameron sat up from the middle of the pile of broken branches, spitting leaves and staring around in astonishment. 'What happened?'

'You fell off the roof,' I said. 'Are you hurt?'

He moved experimentally, making the remains of the tree rustle and creak. 'I don't think so. I fell on the tree. This tree's about a hundred years old. I can't believe it fell just this minute! What are the chances of that happening?'

'Er,' I said. 'Yeah. Do you need a hand?'

'I can manage.' He crawled across the branches until he reached solid ground and stood up in front of me, brushing himself down. There were a few cuts and grazes, but he seemed almost miraculously unhurt.

'I can't believe you didn't break anything,' I said, staring.

'How did that tree fall down?' Cameron insisted. 'The statistical chances must be billions to one!'

'Well,' I said, reluctantly, 'I might have had something to do with that. Lightning is kind of useful for making things fall down. I hope your parents don't mind.'

His mouth dropped open. 'You did that?!

Wow. That's fast work. Wish I'd seen it.'

'You were too busy falling,' I remarked. 'What on earth were you doing up there on the roof?'

'The TV signal has been rubbish for ages,' he said. 'Dad's been promising to get someone in to look at it. I thought I might as well go up and see if I could fix it.'

'But that's really dangerous,' I pointed out. 'You shouldn't go climbing about on roofs. People have special equipment to do that.'

'Yeah, I know,' he said, 'but don't you just want to do something dangerous every now and then? I mean, it's kind of fun!'

I was speechless for a moment. 'But . . . but you hate danger! You're always on about safety!'

He laughed. 'I think maybe I've been kind of boring. Who wants to be safe the whole time?' He glanced up at the roof. 'I nearly had it. I'll go back up and fix it.'

'You are *not* going up there again,' I said firmly. 'I'll run straight to tell your mum if you do.'

'Oh, come *on*. Don't be such a killjoy.'

I reached out to grab his arm as he turned to go. 'Cameron, I mean it. I'll tell on you!'

'Ow.' He pulled back his arm, rubbing it.

'Don't, that hurts.'

I saw the small mark left by the robot's stinger . . . and suddenly something went DING! in my head. The robot! What if it wasn't just a spike? What if . . . what if it was a *needle*, injecting something? Had Cameron been *infected?*!

'Didn't you say you felt ill?' I asked abruptly.

'I'm all right now,' he said.

I took a breath. 'Please, Cameron. Please don't go up on the roof.'

He looked at me from behind his glasses. 'Are you asking me as a friend?'

'What?'

'A friend.' He shuffled awkwardly. 'Are you asking me as a friend?'

I remembered he didn't have many friends, and suddenly I felt sorry for him. 'Yes,' I said. 'I'm asking as a friend. Please don't go up on the roof again.'

He smiled at me. 'All right.'

I hesitated. 'I don't suppose . . . look, could I borrow the—the piskie?'

'It's not a piskie,' he said sadly.

'I know. Sorry. The robot. Could I—could I borrow it?' Given the suspicion that was forming in my mind, it was even more important that we took a closer look.

He sighed. 'All right. Wait a minute.'

Within a minute, he'd gone into the house and reappeared, holding the tiny robot out to me. I took it, being very careful to avoid the silvery stinger. 'Thanks,' I said.

He nodded. 'Don't—don't . . . I mean . . . Look after it, all right?'

'I will.'

He gave a kind of sad shrug and went to close the door.

Impulsively, I said, 'See you later, Cameron. Maybe we can go out and do something later, all of us. Like friends.'

The smile he gave me made me feel guilty and happy all at once.

CHAPTER 9

'He was doing *what?!*' asked Imogen for, like, the fifth time. 'And you did *what* to the tree?!'

'I'm not going through it again,' I said. 'Look, we've got a bigger problem.'

Joe nodded. 'The robot.'

'Am I crazy for thinking it's done something to Cameron?' I asked him.

It had taken me nearly an hour to track them both down, but once I'd shown them the piskie, both Imogen and Joe were prepared to forget our argument and do some proper investigating. 'I need my kit,' Joe said.

'Your what?'

'My kit. You know, my microscope, my notebook, my fingerprint stuff. It's in the caravan.'

I stared at him. 'Are you telling me you brought all that with you on holiday?'

'What?' he said rebelliously. 'You never know when you might need it. And see? We do!'

Annoyingly, when we got to the caravan, we found Cameron's dad Mike there. He'd come over to replace the bulb in the fridge. He and Mum were deep in conversation about the tin mine, so Joe had to go in and grab his kit and bring it out to me and Imogen. It was impossible to find somewhere that wasn't overlooked, so in the end we crouched down on the ground between our caravan and the car, and Imogen was supposed to be on lookout if Mike came out.

The three of us couldn't take our eyes off the robot piskie. Joe was setting up his microscope and pondering my question. 'You mean, Cameron's change in behaviour is down to the sting he got?'

'Yes—don't you think it makes total sense? We *know* how obsessed he is with safety. And now he's clambering over rocks and climbing on roofs—I mean, how could someone change that quickly?'

'You think this isn't a spike?' Joe said. 'It's a needle? And it—what? Injected him with something?'

'Wasps do,' Imogen said. 'They sting you but it's an injection of venom, really. And mosquitoes do, when they bite you. They inject you with something else at the same time, which is what makes it all itchy.'

I stared at her and she blushed. 'What? I know stuff.'

Joe lifted the robot onto the platform of his microscope and peered down the viewfinder. 'I guess there'd have to be a little container of something attached to the needle, if that was the case . . . oh.'

'There is, isn't there?' I guessed.

'Yes.'

I shifted backwards slightly, in case the robot piskie suddenly came to life again and stung us. 'Is it empty?'

'I can't tell.' Joe gazed down the viewfinder for another moment. 'This thing is awesome. Truly mega. It's got so many tiny parts. And how does it operate?'

'You said drones are operated by remote control,' I said. 'Do you think . . . do you think there was someone nearby controlling it?' I shuddered. Had someone been watching us there, in the dark?

Joe shook his head, frustrated. 'I have no idea. I can't imagine it. How would they know when Cameron would come back? You wouldn't hang around all the time waiting, would you? And I can't see an antenna. You'd need one for a radio signal. Maybe—maybe they're more like pigeons.'

'Pigeons?' I repeated, baffled.

'Homing pigeons. Maybe they have a kind of base, and if they're taken away from the base, they automatically follow the signal to get back.'

'Why did it attack us then?' I asked. 'Why didn't it just fly off?'

'I dunno, but this spike is pretty serious. I mean, the thing has been *designed* to attack.'

'Tiny attack drones . . .' said Imogen, wide-eyed. 'It's like something out of *Star Wars*. It can't be real.'

'It's really cool technology,' Joe agreed.

I felt the familiar dread settle in my stomach. 'Technology . . .' I began, but the sound of voices interrupted me, and I stopped as Mike appeared in the caravan doorway.

'Let me know if you want to come on the tour tomorrow,' he said to my mum, who was following a couple of steps behind. Then he caught sight of us. Joe just had time to shove the robot piskie under the car. 'Hello! What are you doing, sitting out here on the gravel?'

'Looking at shells under the microscope,' Joe said promptly, holding up one of Imogen's finds.

I was impressed. Trust my brother to have thought up an excuse in advance!

Mum came down the steps towards us. 'Mike's leading a tour party round the tin mine tomorrow. We should go.'

'Oh,' I said, 'not for me, thanks.'

Joe elbowed me in the ribs and said, 'That would be great! Cameron was telling us all about it.'

Mike laughed. 'That boy! He's obsessed with the tin mine. He's got one of those brains that just soaks up information, you know?'

'Sounds like he'd get on well with Joe,' Mum said, smiling.

'Cameron gets these fixations on things. Can't stop talking about magnetism—or wants to learn Japanese, or—or spends hours down the library reading up about Cornish mythology.'

Imogen, Joe, and I exchanged glances. Piskies, maybe?

Mike sighed. 'The other kids don't understand.

He's been bullied a bit at school because he's different, you know? But underneath he wants friends, like anyone. He just doesn't quite know how to get them in the right way. He upsets people by accident, but he doesn't mean to be unkind.'

'Sometimes it's tough being a parent,' said Mum softly.

I glanced up at her, struck by the tone in her voice. 'It's a shame Dad isn't here,' I said without thinking.

She gave me a sad smile. 'Isn't it? He'd love it. Silly army with their silly rules about holidays. Anyone would think there were wars to be fought somewhere in the world.'

'He'll be back soon, though, won't he?' Joe said.

She nodded. 'Soon.'

'Well,' said Mike, 'I'll be off.'

'You kids coming in?' asked Mum.

'In a minute,' said Joe.

'All right. I'm going to the loo.'

'Too much information, Mum.'

'Sorry!'

As soon as we were alone again, Joe pulled the robot out and put it back under the microscope. 'I'm dying to know which company made this,' he said. 'I mean, it's not the kind of thing you can just order online.'

'Why on earth would you *want* a creepy flying drone with a poisonous stinger?' I asked, repulsed.

He grinned. 'I can think of a few people at school I could use it on . . .'

I rolled my eyes at Imogen.

Joe peered down the viewfinder. 'It's bound to have a maker's mark on it somewhere.'

'Did you look at its wings?' I asked. 'That pattern—don't you think . . . ?'

Imogen said, 'It does look a bit like that spiderweb effect in the CyberSky logo, I suppose. Now that I'm looking properly. But Holly, wings do have a kind of web pattern on them anyway. Veins and things.'

'Yes . . .' said Joe, and he went very still.

'What?' I asked.

'I . . .' He swallowed. 'I think you'd better have a look.'

I don't know if it was something in his voice, but suddenly I had this awful sense of something really bad coming . . . and my powers sprang to the surface, my fingers tingling as I reached for the microscope . . .

CHAPTER 10

My powers disappeared instantly, like they'd been drained out of me.

Joe snatched the microscope from me. 'Holly, can't you **EVER** stop breaking other people's stuff?! What did you *do*?' He peered down the viewfinder. 'You broke the lens. I can't believe it!'

'I'm stressed!' I pleaded. 'I'm really sorry. I'll save up and buy you a new one.'

'You'd better,' he fumed.

Imogen interrupted. 'Guys, guys. The CyberSky logo? It's actually *in* the robot?'

'Yes,' I said. 'It's tiny, but it's there. On one of the middle pieces.'

She stared at me. 'But . . . then . . . Macavity . . .'

Then there was a long pause. My mouth was dry and my head ached. Even though I'd imagined seeing her everywhere; even though

I'd almost convinced myself that Cameron was working for her (I knew that was nuts *now*), I think, deep down, I hoped that maybe I was Just Plain Wrong.

Automatically, I reached for the pager in my pocket.

'Wait,' said Joe, putting down his broken microscope. 'I mean, obviously you have to call him, but hang on a minute.' He looked at the robot. 'This thing is really complicated. It must have taken months, if not years, of work.'

Imogen said, 'So, the mobile phones—the ones that warped our brains—they weren't the only thing she was working on.'

Joe nodded. 'This is a different kind of project. And . . .' he gulped, 'do you remember what Cameron said when he showed it to us?'

'What?' I asked.

'He said he was lucky to get this one away from the others.'

I felt the blood drain from my face. 'The *others*. There are *more*.'

'More drones filled with poison,' whispered Imogen. '*Oh no* . . .'

The pager buzzed in my hand, making me jump so hard I dropped it on the gravel.

'That is **FREAKY**,' said Joe. 'How did he know?'

'Uh . . .' My face felt hot. 'I must have pressed the call button without realizing.' I picked up the pager. The tiny screen showed one thing: a question mark. 'He wants to know what's up.'

The pager was very basic: to anyone who didn't know, it looked like a really old mobile phone, with a keypad and a two-line screen. It only connected to one other pager—the one Steve had in his department.

'What should I say?' I asked. 'There's only really room for a couple of words.'

'We only need one,' Joe said. 'Type **MACAVITY**.'

I typed, with shaking fingers, and pressed 'send'.

There was a pause. And then the pager buzzed again.

TREKENNA CASTLE 6 P.M.

I showed the others. 'Well,' said Joe, 'looks like we've got a rendezvous.'

CHAPTER 11

Mum took one look at us and declared we all needed fish and chips and ice-cream, followed by a swim. 'You look pale and miserable,' she said, 'and I can't think why. We're on holiday! Get your stuff, and let's go and have some fun!'

I had never felt less like having fun. But we couldn't tell Mum what was really going on, and there were six hours to fill before our meeting, so I stretched my face into a happy smile and set off with the others.

It's funny though how, sometimes, when you're pretending to have a good time, you really do end up enjoying yourself. Going for fish and chips and then down to the beach: swimming in the slightly-too-cold water, building sandcastles in the sun, collecting more shells . . . well, I found I was having fun despite my worries. Imogen wailed when her toe got nipped by a crab, and Joe claimed he saw a jellyfish, which made us ALL get out of the water super-fast, but then it turned out to be a plastic bag, which sent Mum off on a rant about how we used too much plastic in our society—and Joe and Imogen and I all looked at each other because Mum is always on some mission or other when it comes to saving the planet.

By the time it got to five o'clock and we were all salty and full of a second round of ice-creams, I'd almost forgotten we had an appointment to keep. 'How are we going to get rid of Mum so we can meet Steve?' Joe whispered to me as we watched the incoming tide break down the walls of our sand village. 'We can't get back to the caravan and tell her we're going out again!'

Help came from an unexpected source. When we got back, Cameron was waiting outside number seventeen. 'Hi!' he said. 'I haven't done any more climbing on the roof, I promise!'

Mum's jaw dropped as I slapped a hand to my head. Cameron had **SUCH** a problem with blurting things out! 'On the roof?' she said faintly.

'Oh, I'm fine,' Cameron said airily. 'Holly saved—'

'It's lovely to see you again,' I broke in desperately. Before we knew it, Cameron would have told Mum about my powers. 'What are you doing here?'

'Oh—well, earlier you said we might all go out later. As friends. And now is later. And so I'm here.'

Mum's face softened, and I could tell she was thinking about what Mike had said about Cameron being bullied. 'That's so lovely,' she said. 'Why don't the four of you go for a walk together while I get tea ready? Be back in about half an hour?'

I could see Joe mentally calculating how long it would take us to get to Trekenna Castle and back again. 'Er . . . maybe forty minutes,' he said.

Mum gave him a puzzled glance. 'Where are you planning on going?'

'Up to the town,' Joe said promptly. 'I want Cameron to show me where I can buy some batteries tomorrow.'

'Oh, that's easy,' said Cameron. 'We don't need to go to town for that.'

'Yes we do,' said Joe firmly. 'Come on!'

Cameron trailed out of the park after us, still

arguing that the shops were all closed and there was nothing to see in town at this time on a Sunday. When we got out onto the road, we all stopped. 'We're not going into town,' I told Cameron.

'Well, good,' he said, 'because I was thinking we could go climbing over the rocks. There's this cliff-face bit that people never dare to climb, and I think it'd be cool to go up there!'

I rolled my eyes. 'We're going to Trekenna Castle.'

He looked baffled. 'What? Why?'

Joe took my arm and muttered, 'He can't come with us. What will Steve say?'

'He's our alibi,' I muttered back. 'And he's been stung. He's evidence.'

Joe sighed. 'I suppose so. All right.' He turned to Cameron. 'You can't tell anyone where we're going. And you mustn't tell anyone what happens.'

Cameron's eyes opened wide. 'Is it superhero stuff?'

'Yes,' I said.

Imogen said reassuringly, 'Don't worry, Cameron, we'll be perfectly safe.'

His face fell. 'Doesn't sound like much fun.'

Trekenna Castle was about fifteen minutes' walk from the caravan site. The name made it sound really grand, but actually there was no castle there. There must have been one once, but now it was just a big clearing on a bit of a hill. It was a weird place to meet Steve, but I guessed he'd picked it because there were no houses nearby.

'Did you bring the piskie?' I asked Joe suddenly.

He looked scornful. 'You don't imagine I'd have left it behind, do you? I've been carrying it in my swim bag all day. I stuck a bit of cork I found on the beach onto the stinger so it couldn't do any damage. Now it's in my pocket.'

I could see, as we crossed a field and approached Trekenna Castle, that the wide open space was completely empty. Where was Steve? I guessed you could get a Land Rover up here, and kept looking around to see if there was anything coming.

We reached the top of the mound and stopped. 'He's late,' Joe said, checking his watch.

'He's probably been doing something top secret,' Imogen said. 'You know, in the top secrety way he has.'

'What's that noise?' asked Cameron.

A deep, low thrumming filled the air. 'Helicopter,' Joe said, looking up.

A tiny dot was approaching from the coast. 'Coast guard,' said Imogen.

Joe shook his head. 'No way. Secret government agent. It just has to be.' I could tell by the tone of his voice that he was practically bursting with excitement, and I have to say, I was kind of impressed too!

The sleek black helicopter reached us within seconds, and then we were all running off the mound, yelling to each other, and my hair blew into my face and I felt like I might actually be blown off my feet as it descended to land lightly on the grass.

'**WOW**!' said Cameron. At least, I think that's what he said, but I could only see his mouth moving because the sound of the rotors was so loud.

Then the thrumming dropped, and the rotors slowed, and I could see a man climbing out.

Steve—the man we'd first met walking his big dog, Thor, outside the CyberSky building in Bluehaven. The man we'd thought was crazy because he kept talking about aliens—and then he turned out to be the real deal, running a secret department that investigated all kinds of unusual happenings.

He grinned at us as we ran over, his brown eyes crinkling at the corners. His mop of black hair was all blown over to one side by the wind, and it made me giggle. He didn't look anything like a secret agent, but I'd seen him in authority after the events at CyberSky, and there was a steely determination under the casual friendliness.

'Hi, kids. This had better be good, dragging me all the way down from Scotland.' Then his eyebrows drew together in a frown, as Cameron ran up to join us. 'Who's this?'

'Cameron,' Cameron said helpfully. 'I live here. Is that an Augusta Power?'

Steve raised one eyebrow. 'It's had a few modifications, but yes.'

'Can I fly it?' Before Steve could protest, Cameron had yanked open the cabin door and was climbing in next to the pilot.

'No!' Steve reached in and grabbed his T-shirt, pulling him back out of the machine. 'What do you think you're doing? This isn't a toy!'

'Well, it is, really,' Cameron said. 'Just a toy for

grown-ups.'

Steve looked at him for a moment and then grinned. 'You're right there. But you can't fly it. It's worth more pocket money than you'll earn in a lifetime. And I'd be fired on the spot.'

'Better not stand on a spot then,' Cameron told him earnestly.

Steve's eyes narrowed.

'Cameron's a bit . . . er . . . literal,' Imogen jumped in hastily. 'It's just the way he talks.'

'What's all this about?' Steve asked. 'I haven't got much time.'

Joe pulled out the robot piskie. 'It's about this, basically.'

Steve took it from him and whistled. 'This is a neat bit of kit. Why's it got a cork stuck on the end of an arm?'

'That's not an arm; it's a hypodermic needle,' Joe told him. 'We think it's carrying poison.'

'I got stung,' added Cameron helpfully. 'It's my piskie—I found it.'

'Piskie?' Steve looked baffled.

'Cameron thought it was a Cornish piskie,' I explained. 'And then it stung him, and I zapped it, and then we realized it was a robot.'

'And then I looked at it under my microscope,'

Joe went on, 'and it's . . . it's got the CyberSky logo on it.'

In an instant, everything about Steve seemed to sharpen, like he'd suddenly come into focus. 'Are you sure?' he asked, and even his voice sounded different.

'Positive. It's really small, but it's there.'

'What kind of poison?' Steve asked.

'We're not sure, but . . .' Joe glanced at Cameron, 'it makes people behave differently.'

'I'm fine!' said Cameron.

'You're dangerous,' I told him.

'When we arrived,' Imogen said, 'Cameron went on about health and safety and not climbing over the rocks or anything. His mum said he's always been obsessed with rules and keeping safe.'

Cameron shook his head. 'The old me was really boring.'

'And then he got stung, and now he keeps trying to do dangerous things,' I said, 'like climbing on the roof of his house to fix the TV aerial.'

'And . . .' Imogen said, 'he said there are more of them. More robots.'

'There are!' exclaimed Cameron. 'Hundreds

more! Like bats! I was really lucky to catch this one!' He beamed.

Steve paused for a moment, thinking. Then he said, 'Right. I'll need to get this back to the lab. And I think'—he looked Cameron up and down—'we'll need a blood sample.'

Cameron stuck out an arm enthusiastically. 'Go for it! Can I watch?'

CHAPTER 12

I found it really hard to get to sleep that night. Watching Steve take off in his helicopter with the piskie and the blood sample made my heart sink. I don't know what I'd expected—he couldn't exactly hang around in Cornwall and come piskie-hunting, could he? And he did say he was doing something important in Scotland. But still . . . he was the only grown-up we could trust, and now that we knew Professor Macavity was really involved, it felt like we needed a grown-up around.

Steve had taken me aside before he left. 'Talk to Joe,' he said in a low voice. 'I know it must be hard, having a younger brother as a mentor, but he has good ideas. And Imogen's a bright kid, too. Use your support network.'

'But we're on our own,' I said, trying not to sound too gutted.

Steve put a hand on my shoulder. 'I'm only a bleep away. Well, a few hours by bleep. But I can get help to you faster if you need it. Come to think of it . . .' He glanced off towards the sea, and then grinned. 'Tell you what: I'll assign someone down here to keep an eye on you.'

'Who?' I asked.

'You'll see him when you need to,' Steve said reassuringly. 'Now listen. I want you guys to sit tight until I've got results back from the lab on the venom and the blood sample, all right? Don't go off looking for danger.'

'What do we do about Cameron?' I asked.

Steve shook his head. 'I have no idea! Try not to let him jump off any cliffs, okay? And whatever you do, stay away from where he found them.'

I nodded, but it was only after Steve had gone that I realized I didn't actually *know* where Cameron had found the piskie. And when I tried to ask him on the walk back to the caravan park, he ignored me completely. Instead, he insisted on walking in the middle of the road and jumping to the side at the last minute whenever a car approached, missing him by centimetres and blaring its horn. Keeping him safe was going to be IMPOSSIBLE!

And who was this mysterious person that Steve was going to ask to look after us? Why had Steve grinned when he mentioned him?

Too many thoughts whirled round my head as I lay wide awake ...

'Wakey wakey!' Joe bounced onto the end of the bed, making it creak alarmingly. I blinked, groggily. Had I been asleep? What time was it?

My brother was looking ridiculously perky. 'We need to do some training today,' he said. 'I've been planning some exercises for you.'

'I'm tired,' I complained. On the other side of the bed, Imogen mumbled something about holidays that were supposed to be restful.

'Oh, come on,' Joe said. 'Mum's got a migraine, so we have to go out anyway. It's a good time to get some training in. Because the chances are, we're going to come up against You-Know-Who before too long ...'

'Voldemort?' I said sarcastically, pulling the duvet over my head.

Joe tugged on it. 'Holly. You know who I mean!'

I sat up, irritated. 'Oh, so NOW you're all fired up about her? When I've been saying for ages that she's got some secret plan we don't know about, and how she's probably just around the corner, and you laughed at me and said I was imagining things?'

Joe had the decency to look a bit embarrassed. 'Yeah, okay, so I was wrong about that. But this is the perfect opportunity. And you *wanted* to do more training, didn't you?'

I sighed. 'Yes. Oh, all right. Just let me wake up a bit first.'

I suggested going back to Trekenna Castle for training, but Joe disagreed. 'Too exposed,' he said. 'We can be seen from a long way off. We need somewhere more sheltered.'

'Cameron would know the best place,' Imogen said.

'No way,' I said, but Joe thought it was a good idea.

'We can keep an eye on him at the same time,' he said.

So in the end we called for Cameron, who (to my relief) was still alive and eager to watch some superhero training. Half an hour later, we were in a small cove on the beach, completely hidden from the clifftop above and only reached by a winding path over the rocks.

'FOCUS ...' SAID JOE

HOLLY'S POWERS WERE EASILY UP TO THIS!

HOLLY CHANNELLED HER POWERS AND SLOWLY LIFTED OFF THE GROUND INSIDE A BALL OF ELECTRICITY!

BUT CAMERON WASN'T GOOD AT FOLLOWING INSTRUCTIONS!

CHAPTER 13

'You're our . . . what?' I said blankly, but Joe jumped in.

'You're the guy Steve's sent.'

The young man grinned. 'That's right. Secret agent, super-sleuth, and now child liaison officer. I have to say, I wasn't expecting my career to go quite like this.'

'How did you find us?' asked Imogen.

The man cast her a look. 'Are you *seriously* asking me that?' His voice was teasing. 'I can find anything. Anywhere. Except my own keys, in the morning.' He burst out laughing.

'What's your name?' I asked.

He stuck out a hand and I noticed he was wearing black nail varnish. 'Maverick. Mav for short.'

'Maverick?' I said, shaking his hand. 'Is that your real name?'

'Course not. It's my code name. But I'm not telling you my real name.' He leaned forward and whispered, 'It's safer that way.'

'I'm Cameron,' Cameron said, bounding forward like a puppy and shaking Mav's hand. 'That was so cool, how you got down here so fast! Can I have a go on your rope?'

'Sure,' said Mav. 'When you're eighteen.'

Cameron's face fell, and Mav laughed again. 'You must be the kid with a danger addiction, right? The one who got stung?'

'That's right,' I said. 'And this is Imogen, my best friend, and Joe—my brother.'

Mav nodded. 'I've read your files. You guys have done some pretty awesome work already. I've got news for you on your robot fairy.'

'Piskie,' Cameron corrected him.

'Yeah, that. Well, you're right—it's definitely one of Macavity's. We didn't know anything about it. No idea she was working on this at the same time as all the stuff that was going down in Bluehaven. We don't know why *here*, either. But she does like to try new tech out in remote villages, it seems.'

'Do you know where she is?' I asked, afraid of the answer.

Mav rubbed the back of his neck. 'Between you and me, it's all a bit embarrassing. We were keeping tabs on her, but she's super-sneaky.'

'You *lost* her?' Joe said.

'Yeah. Don't tell Steve I told you. He yelled a LOT at the surveillance peeps when he found out.' Mav gave me a look. 'Seems he thinks a lot of you.'

I blushed. 'What does he want us to do?'

'Nothing.' Mav seemed a bit disappointed by this. 'The lab people have analysed the venom. They think it's a toxin derived from some plant or other. It makes people crave danger. They put their lives at risk. Climbing on roofs and suchlike.' He glanced at Cameron. 'It's pretty powerful. Hard to resist. Your blood cells have binding agents attached that are repressing neural signals.'

'Huh?' said Cameron.

'You have weird blood.'

'Oh.'

'Does it wear off?' asked Joe.

'They don't think so. Could be permanent. Which means we need an antidote. They're working on it.' He smiled at Cameron. 'We'll get you back to normal.'

'I don't want to be back to normal,' Cameron sulked. 'I was boring.'

'Well, whatever. But you're to enjoy your holiday, okay? I'm on the lookout for Macavity, and you kids are to have a fun time. When we've got more news for you, I'll come and find you again, but for now, just stay out of trouble. There's no evidence that this project is anything to do with you, Electrigirl. So leave the sleuthing to me, and get on with holiday stuff. Sandcastles, swimming . . . er.' He looked blank for a moment. 'That sort of thing.'

'Oh,' I said, not sure whether to be relieved or disappointed.

'Keep up the training though,' Maverick said. 'Especially that net thing. That's beautiful work.'

'Oh. Thanks.'

He thought for a moment. 'Listen, I'm going to give you my mobile number. Call me if you spot anything. But just for emergencies, okay? I don't want to know if you've run out of ice-cream.'

Joe took the little business card and grinned at him. 'We'll get our own. You want some too?'

Mav laughed. 'Coffee flavour, thanks. I need all the caffeine I can get.' He clipped the rope back onto his harness, pressed a button on his belt, and shot off the ground up to the top of the cliff, letting out a whoop as he went.

We stared.

'Whoa,' said Cameron quietly. 'When I grow up, I want to be HIM.'

'I'm sorry your mum isn't well,' Mike said. 'Julie gets migraines sometimes. I must get her to pop round later with the herbal tea she takes for it.'

'Thanks,' I said.

He smiled at us. 'It's great that the three of you are joining us, though. This mine is a slice of history, as they say.'

Joe, Imogen, and I had joined Mike and Cameron and a small group of people at the tin mine, which was about a twenty-minute walk from the caravan site. I hadn't wanted to come. In fact, I'd rather have gone climbing about on a roof than go down the mine. But after Maverick had gone, we'd headed back to the caravan only to discover Mum was still lying down in darkness. 'Sorry, kids,' she said weakly. 'I'm being rubbish.'

'It's not your fault,' I told her.

'I don't want you running about unsupervised,' Mum whispered. 'I promised Imogen's mum. She rang while you were out. Your gran's doing okay in the hospital, Imogen.'

Imogen looked relieved. 'Thanks.'

'Why don't you go down that old tin mine?' Mum suggested. 'Mike will keep an eye on you. You could tell him how sorry I am that I can't come today.'

'Oh . . .' I said, my mind swirling in a panic. 'Oh, that's okay, we'll find something else to do.' Not the mine! Not underground!

But Mum had fixed me with a stern glare— made even sterner by the pain lines across her forehead. 'Please, Holly. Do as you're asked. I need to know that you're being properly supervised.'

What could I say?

Cameron had bounced with delight when we told him the plan. 'It's cool!' he said. 'You'll LOVE it!'

'No,' I said. 'I won't.'

'No, honestly, you will.'

'Honestly,' I said. 'I really won't. I don't do dark enclosed spaces. Especially underground.'

'It's not dark,' he said triumphantly. 'There are

lights. Ha!'

I exchanged glances with Imogen. She reached for my hand and squeezed it. 'We'll be okay,' she whispered to me. 'Just keep calm.'

Cameron had led the way, talking non-stop to Joe about granite and veins and something called a stope, while I tried to control my buzzing brain.

And now here we were. There was one huge building still standing, and two walls of a second. A tall thin chimney rose up behind it, pointing straight into the blue sky. A family of mum, dad, and twin boys was peering at a guide book, and another man had come on his own with what looked like a really expensive camera. To the left of the buildings, a lift shaft poked up out of the ground, the metal cage open and waiting.

Cameron was hopping from foot to foot like an excited grasshopper.

'Right,' said Mike, 'before we go down, there are a few safety things I need to go through.'

I took a breath and let it out slowly. You can do this, I told myself. These mine tunnels have been fine for over a hundred years. They won't collapse on you. You won't get stuck. It'll be fine.

We were given hard hats to wear. Joe grinned in delight and immediately started pulling stupid faces. Even Imogen smiled. I just couldn't. The hat reminded me of the metal helmet I'd worn in the basement of the CyberSky HQ, when Professor Macavity had strapped me into her awful Machine and I'd been drained of all my powers. My hands trembled as I put it on, and I felt angry with myself. Get a grip, Holly!

We all got into the metal cage, and then Mike pressed a switch and we began to descend. I closed my eyes, concentrating on my breathing. The last thing I needed was for my powers to switch on! Goodness knows what would happen with all this metal in the rock . . .

Mike was talking about how the miners would find a vein of tin or copper on the surface and then dig straight down to follow it. Cameron kept interrupting, adding in bits his dad had forgotten. Mike didn't seem to mind. I suppose he was used to it.

'It goes a long way down, doesn't it?' whispered Imogen to me.

'Yes,' I said, biting my lip.

'How are you doing?'

'Not all that well,' I admitted.

The lift hit the bottom of the shaft with a clank.

'Right,' said Mike. 'Follow me, but remember that these tunnels are very narrow. Make sure you follow me, and don't go off down any side passages because they're not all safe. As you go, look at the walls of the tunnel and you'll see the vein of tin running through it. That's what the miners dug out with hammers and explosives, and when we get back to the surface, I'll show you how the tin was extracted from the rock. Ready? Off we go, then.'

The tunnel was narrow and not very tall, and I hated it. Hated every second; hated concentrating on putting one foot in front of the other. It wasn't too dark because there were electric lamps every few metres, but I kept bumping into the wall because my legs felt wobbly. Worse still, my fingers went tingly when they came into contact with the tin in the walls, as though there were some kind of primeval electrical energy running through the hills . . . and then something happened

SORT OF BY ACCIDENT . . .

Sulking, I switched off my powers and felt fear grip me again. How long before we reached the next mine shaft and had a bit more room?!

Not long, thankfully. Within another minute, I was clambering out of the tunnel and into a much wider area. Mike was standing in the middle of the group, pointing upwards. 'Ah, good!' he said, smiling. 'Not lost anyone yet then. If you look up, you can see another shaft—this one is much shallower than the one we came down because the ground outside has sloped downwards.'

I felt slightly dizzy looking up. A narrow rectangle of light showed at the top of a chimney of darkness. A metal ladder was fixed to the side of the chimney. 'People actually climbed up and down that?' Imogen whispered.

Mike heard her. 'Yes—and carrying all kinds of equipment, too. This is one of the smaller mines, older than some of the rest. The miners who worked down here did so with hammers and pickaxes, and any stone they hacked out of the walls, they had to lift to the surface somehow. It was hard work. And if you look at the walls, you can see holes about an inch across. They used man-powered drills: two men taking it in turns to hit a metal peg held by a third man, who twisted it at the same time. Then when the hole was deep enough, they packed it with gunpowder and lit a fuse.'

'Bet they didn't live long,' said the man with the camera cheerfully.

The twin boys giggled.

'You're right,' Mike said. 'The life expectancy was around forty. Anyone who worked down here was at risk of all kinds of things. Tunnel collapse, injuries from flying rock chips, eyesight problems, hearing problems—not to mention the arsenic and other nasties in the dust they breathed in.'

'Arsenic?' echoed one of the boys. 'Cool!' His mother nudged him and told him not to be disrespectful.

'You'll see there's another passageway leading off this shaft,' Mike said, pointing behind Joe. 'So there's the one we came up, the one we're going to go down next, and that one. That's a very narrow one, set on a diagonal because the miners were following the angle of the vein of tin. It opens out a bit further on, but it's a very tight squeeze, so we won't be going down there today.'

I glanced across at the narrow slit of the opening and felt thankful to be spared an even narrower tunnel. And then I realized Cameron was looking right at me with a kind of burning intensity . . .

I frowned. 'What is it?' I mouthed at him.

He beamed, with the widest smile I'd ever seen him give. His teeth shone white in the lamplight. And then he lifted his arms, just a little, and flapped his hands up and down.

My breath stopped in my throat as I felt a sudden heavy realization sink into me.

The piskies were down that tunnel!

CHAPTER 16

I went cold all over. Maverick had told us specifically to stay out of trouble. We weren't supposed to be looking for the rest of the robots. We were supposed to stay safe. We KNEW Cameron was a danger-nut, and yet we'd blindly agreed to come down here with him! No wonder he'd been hopping like a cricket up top! He couldn't wait to get us into the mine!

'What is it?' Imogen whispered urgently. 'You look like you've seen a ghost. Are you sick?'

Quickly, I whispered in her ear. She went pale. 'Are you sure?' Then she glanced across at Cameron. 'You're right. He *wanted* us to come down here and put ourselves in danger!'

Joe was at my shoulder. 'He gets a thrill out of dangerous situations. We should have guessed.'

'What do we do now?'

Mike was answering questions from the

other people on the tour and didn't seem to have noticed that the three of us were holding back. Cameron took a step towards us.

'Are you crazy?' I hissed.

His eyes were gleaming. 'Come on, I'll show them to you! Follow me!'

'No—' I said, but Cameron had already disappeared into the dark opening!

'We have to go after him,' Joe said urgently. 'Before he wakes up all the other piskies. I'll go—I've got a torch. You two should get the rest of the people out of here.'

He took a step into the dark, narrow opening. My heart pounded. 'It should be me,' I said without thinking, and almost swallowed my own tongue. I didn't want to go in there—what was I saying?! 'I'm the one with powers.'

'Yeah,' said Joe, 'and look how dangerous they could be down here! You could cause a rockfall.'

'What if he wakes up the piskies?' I countered. 'How are you going to protect yourself?'

Joe hesitated.

'Look, I know I'm not exactly safe,' I went

on in a low tone, 'but Cameron is *dangerous* and he's walking into a nest of deadly stinging robots. What are you going to do, show them your Batman comics?'

He glared at me. 'Fine.' He stepped out of the tunnel. 'Just try not to *die*, all right?'

'It's not high on my list,' I snapped back.

'Don't fight,' Imogen said with tears in her eyes. 'He just doesn't want you to get hurt.'

'Well, he's got a funny way of showing it,' I said, unwilling to let go of my temper. If I could stay cross, I wouldn't be frightened. 'Go and get the others out.' I turned my back on them and stepped into the tunnel. That flipping Cameron! I'd drag him out of here if I had to . . .

The tunnel was barely wide enough for me to squeeze along, and I kept banging my knees on the walls and tripping over my own feet. That kept me irritated, too, but the further along I went, the darker and quieter it seemed, and the closer the walls.

MY FINGERS TINGLED,

and I put out my hands to steady myself on either side . . .

THE TUNNEL WAS LONGER THAN HOLLY EXPECTED.

CHAPTER 17

I stared up at the clear sky.

'Was that all of them?' Joe said in a voice that wasn't quite steady.

'I don't know.'

'What's happened to Cameron?'

'I don't care.' My face felt hot and tight. 'We have to find the piskies and destroy them.'

'Why did they wake up?' Joe asked. 'Did Cameron do it?'

I bit my lip. 'Not exactly.' How could I tell him it was my fault—that their eyes had opened when my electricity touched them?

To my relief, Joe didn't ask any more. 'We can't leave him down here.'

I looked at him, frustrated. He glared back.

'Oh, all *right*,' I grumbled.

Joe went to the opening of the narrow tunnel and called, 'Cameron! Cameron, you okay? Can you hear me?'

There was a distant shout, and then the sound of footsteps getting closer. Cameron emerged, covered in dust and beaming from ear to ear. 'Wasn't that **AMAZING**?' he exclaimed.

I clenched my fists to stop myself punching him. 'Amazing?!' I repeated. 'We've just set loose a whole swarm of deadly robots!'

'Don't worry,' Cameron said cheerfully, 'there's still loads back there in the cave.'

My jaw hit the floor. Well, you know, not for real. But I was speechless.

'Where did everyone go?' asked Cameron, looking around.

'Imogen pretended to faint,' Joe explained. 'So your dad had to cut the tour short. I told him you'd taken Holly down that tunnel and he was really cross, but then Imogen did another faint and he had to take everyone back up to the surface.'

Cameron was disappointed. 'I wanted to show him the piskies.'

'Cameron,' I said, through gritted teeth, 'the piskies are *dangerous*. Can you imagine what would happen if lots of people got stung? Everyone wanting to take risks? Putting themselves in danger all the time?'

'Oh, lighten up, Holly,' said Cameron. 'Taking risks is fun! You're just jealous because superheroes have to be all goody-goody.'

Joe held me back. 'We've got to go,' he said. 'We have to find that swarm. Can you blast them, Holly?'

I hesitated. 'There were an awful lot. I can try.'

'Let's go.' Joe cast a glance at Cameron. 'We've got important things to do now. Don't go climbing any more roofs, or Holly might not be there to save you.'

'I won't need saving,' Cameron said confidently. 'I know what I'm doing.'

I was so relieved to be out in the fresh air again. I didn't think I'd ever like being underground!

Mike and the other members of the tour party were clustered around Imogen, who was sitting on the ground looking a bit embarrassed. 'Holly!' she said.

'Hi!' I said. 'Are you all right? I hear you fainted.'

'I was just suggesting I should take her to the local hospital to get her checked out,' Mike said.

I felt bad for fibbing to him. 'Oh, I'm sure she'll be fine. She faints all the time, don't you, Imogen?'

'Er . . . yeah. Yeah. Low blood pressure.'

'Oh.' Mike stood up. 'Well, if you're sure. I do think you should go back to the caravan and rest, though.'

'I'll take them,' Cameron offered. I fumed. It was his fault we were in this mess! If he hadn't gone down that tunnel . . . ! *And if you hadn't followed him*, a little voice in my mind said. I shook my head. There was no point in blaming myself now. What mattered was what we did next.

We handed back our helmets and headed quickly out of the gates. I filled Imogen in as we went. 'They're loose?' she said in alarm. 'How many of them?'

'A lot,' I said grimly. 'We have to find them.'

'Should we call Maverick?'

I hesitated. We'd had strict instructions to stay out of trouble—I cringed at the thought of Steve knowing what had happened. 'Not yet,' I said. 'Let's see if we can fix it.' Joe opened his mouth to disagree. 'We haven't got time,' I said quickly, and he shut it again.

'All right,' said Imogen. 'Where should we look?'

'They're programmed to attack people,' Joe said. 'So they'd go where there are lots of people.'

'Lots of people . . .' I looked up at the sky. There wasn't a cloud to be seen, and it was a beautifully hot day. 'The beach!'

'Come on!' yelled Cameron, setting off. 'I know a short cut over the rocks!'

Even before we reached the beach, I could tell we were going in the right direction. Screams and shouts were almost drowned out by a loud buzzing. The four of us raced towards the dunes, and stopped when we got to the edge of the sand ...

As my powers faded again, I became uncomfortably aware of the number of people staring at me. 'Oh . . .'

A child came running up. 'That was totally *awesome*!' she shouted, her face alight. I noticed a puncture mark on her arm. 'Are you a superhero? A real one?'

I didn't know what to say! 'Er . . . well . . . sort of . . .' I mumbled. Maybe it was time to seriously consider some kind of disguise for moments like this!

A faint humming reached my ears and I frowned. It sounded like—

A motorbike screeched to a halt at the top of the nearest dune, showering sand over the three people standing closest. Maverick, clad in his black gear, pulled off his helmet to reveal a brightly coloured bandana tied around his head. 'All right, folks, party's over!' he shouted.

I turned to my brother, raising my eyebrows. He looked guilty. 'All right, so I called him! I thought we might need some help.'

'Gather round!' Maverick called. 'I'm from Homeland Security, and we've had a technology breach. If you could come this way, I'll explain what's going to happen next.'

People shuffled forward, rubbing arms and legs and staring, puzzled, at Maverick.

I was puzzled, too. What was he going to tell them?

Mav grinned at us and gave a weird kind of wink. I frowned. It looked like he'd blinked both eyes at us instead of just one, like when a child tries to do it. Definitely at odds with his super-cool persona. 'Now,' he called to the crowd, reaching for something in one of his many jacket pockets, 'I understand you'll have a lot of questions, but this projection should help to answer them!' He threw something small into the air. About five hundred pairs of eyes followed it.

Joe grabbed my arm, hard. I turned. 'Ow! That—'

There was a blinding flash from above. Joe had his eyes tightly screwed shut. I whirled round again, pulling free. 'What was *that*?'

Maverick was coming down the dune towards us. The people, gathered in an untidy bunch, looked around, rubbing their eyes and reaching out to hug each other.

Imogen reached for my hand. 'You're my *best* friend, Holly. You know that, don't you?'

'Er . . .' I said, somewhat surprised.

Cameron took my other hand. 'You're my best friend, too. And Imogen. And Joe. Isn't life *amazing*?'

'*Maverick*,' I said, 'what did you DO?'

He grinned at me as I tried to let go of Cameron's hand. 'It's a kind of neural tranquillizer. It uses light receptors in the eyes to trigger synaptic responses in the emotional cortex.'

'*What*?'

'It makes people feel happy and spaced out when they look at it,' he said.

Joe was chuckling. '*Cool*. I love it.'

'How did you know not to look?' I asked him.

'Mav signalled to us,' he said. 'Didn't you see it?'

'That was a signal?' I said. 'I thought he was trying to wink!'

My brother rolled his eyes. 'Good thing I'm around. We can't have Electrigirl spacing out in times of need.'

'Speaking of which,' said Mav, surveying the beach, 'it looks like you've been busy.'

The sand was still littered with the metal bodies

of the piskie robots, but the holidaymakers showed not the slightest interest in them, heading slowly back to their towels and bags, laughing and hugging each other along the way.

'Clear-up time,' Mav said. From another pocket he produced a tiny bag. He blew into it, and suddenly the whole thing expanded to about two metres across. 'Synthetic net,' he explained to me. 'It's a polymer—'

'Whatever,' I said, shaking free of Imogen and Cameron, who instantly took each other's hands and sat down on the sand to gaze at the sea.

Joe, Mav, and I worked quickly, picking up the piskies as carefully as we could and dropping them into his bag. When the beach was finally clear, Mav straightened up and tied the bag tightly. 'Just in case any of them suddenly come back to life,' he said, grinning. 'The bad ones always come back to life just when you least expect it. I've learned that from watching horror films.'

'How are you going to carry them off?' Joe asked, looking at the motorbike, which didn't seem big enough to support the enormous bag of piskies.

'Oh, I'll call for a pickup,' Mav said. 'Steve'll be delighted we've got so many more specimens to work on. Though it's a shame they spiked so many people while they were out.'

'Er, yeah . . .' I said. 'Sorry.'

He looked at me more kindly. 'Want to tell me what happened?'

Joe and I explained. I even awkwardly confessed what had triggered the wake-up, but Mav seemed less interested in that than their numbers. 'Whoa! You mean this isn't all of them?'

I shook my head. 'Nowhere near.'

'This is big, man.' Mav sounded almost admiring. 'I mean, you've got to hand it to the woman. Nutty as a fruitcake she may be, but she's got ambition!'

CHAPTER 19

It was an hour later, and the four of us and Mav were sitting outside a sea-front cafe in Polcarrow. Within ten minutes of Mav calling for backup, a black four-wheel-drive had roared up the dunes. A beautiful Chinese woman with sleek black hair and sunglasses hopped out, hefted the bag of piskies into the boot and drove off, with a nod to Mav, who looked faintly disappointed that she hadn't stopped to chat. 'That's Lin,' he said with a sigh. 'She speaks seven languages and is a black belt in karate. She once laid me out flat in training. Happy days.' Joe and I exchanged a glance. Lin sounded awesome! I made a mental note to ask for karate lessons when we got home.

And now we were just finishing the ice-creams and fizzy drinks Mav had insisted on buying for us. I'd thought he was being kind, but then I noticed that his ice-cream was about twice the size of everyone else's—and it was all coffee flavour. With a cup of coffee on the side.

'Isn't it bad for you?' I asked.

Mav waved his spoon at me. 'Vital. I can't function without caffeine. Seriously. I have to have an espresso just to get me out of bed in the morning.'

Imogen and Cameron had stopped holding hands and being goofy and now just looked mildly embarrassed. 'Now that the neural thingy has worn off,' I said, 'won't the people on the beach remember me blasting all the piskies?'

'Nah,' Mav said. 'It messes with your short-term memory a bit. Anything that happened on the beach will seem like a dream, if they remember it at all.' He took another spoonful of ice-cream. 'It's a clever little thing, but it's only temporary. Wipes out a few minutes, that's all.'

'Did you blast all the piskies then?' Imogen asked, puzzled.

'Er,' I said, 'yeah—I did, mostly. Don't you remember?'

'Yes. No. Not sure.' She grinned at me. 'Well done.'

'No word from Steve yet?' Joe asked.

Mav patted his pocket. 'I'll tell you as soon as I get anything. Though I don't think he's going to be thrilled about this.'

'No . . .' I looked down guiltily.

'Well, I think it's brilliant,' Imogen said. 'I mean, last time, I was strapped into an evil machine and had my mind warped, and I didn't even know what was going on until it was nearly over. This time, I'm in at the start, and we've got a real chance of bringing down Macavity!'

I stared at her. 'What are you talking about? What chance? We don't even know where she is!'

'We'll find her,' Imogen said confidently. 'And when we do . . . **BAM**!' She smacked her spoon on the table.

'What, you're going to hit her with a spoon?' I said sarcastically.

Imogen shot me a look. 'No, we're going to bring her DOWN. Permanently.'

A strange suspicion crossed my mind. 'Imogen, are you okay? You sound . . . different.'

'What do you mean? I'm fine.'

'She's right,' Cameron said. 'This professor isn't going to mess with us. Not now we're invincible.'

I groaned. '*Please* tell me you haven't been stung, Imogen.'

She shifted on her seat. 'Holly, I'm fine. It hardly even hurt.'

'Show me,' I demanded.

She gave an exasperated sigh and stood up. On her right knee, a red mark showed up against her pale skin. 'I feel fine,' she insisted.

I glanced at Mav. 'Not surprising,' he said to me. 'Given the number of piskies swarming around. You were lucky not to be stung, too.'

'Those piskies!' Joe shook his head. 'They need to be destroyed. Holly, you should go down into the mine and just blow them all up. Then they can't do any more damage.'

I felt sick and dizzy. 'Oh no, Joe, not you too . . .'

'Hey,' Joe said, 'who fancies trying to walk along that railing over there?' He pointed to where a thin rail ran along the edge of the esplanade.

'Me!' Imogen and Cameron shouted at the same minute.

Then all three of them got up and ran across the road, without even bothering to look for traffic. There was a squealing of brakes and some very rude language from a driver, but fortunately no screams of pain.

I put my head in my hands. 'I can't look. They've all been infected. What am I going to do?'

The James Bond theme tune suddenly started playing from Mav's jacket. He reached in and pulled out a slim black phone. 'Yup?' he said.

Across the road, Imogen and Joe were fighting to be the first onto the railing, whereas Cameron had run along to the next break in the wall and was practising jumping across the gap. He fell heavily, grazing his leg, but in the next minute had bounded to his feet and was trying again. I covered my eyes.

'Yeah, I know,' Mav was saying, 'there's loads of them. But at least you've got more venom to help synthesize the antidote . . . I dunno how many people were on the beach. Maybe four hundred? Most of them got stung, I'd guess, before Holly zapped the robots . . . Yeah, that's right, more of them down the mine . . . Are you *sure*?'

I looked up, aware that the tone in Maverick's voice had changed. 'No,' he said, 'it's not that

I don't think she can do it, but . . . yeah, I'll tell her. What? . . . Oh. Um, I used the visual tranquillizer.' He held the phone away from his ear, wincing as the voice on the other end suddenly became loud enough for me to hear that it was very, very angry. In a small pause, Mav interjected, 'But it's not *permanent*. I *meant* to sign it out . . . Yeah. Bye.' He hung up and shrugged ruefully at me. 'They don't like me borrowing stuff from the lab without asking. I wasn't authorized to use the tranq, and now I've got to fill out a report. I hate writing.'

'What do you have to tell me?' I asked. 'What don't you think I can do?'

For the first time since we'd met, Maverick looked uncomfortable. 'Look, you could just say you're not going to do it. Though obviously that might cause a bit of bad feeling—'

'What am I supposed to do?' I demanded.

Mav sighed. 'They want you to go into the mines and destroy the rest of the robots. First thing tomorrow morning.'

CHAPTER 20

Mum was up and about the next morning, her migraine much improved. She felt my forehead anxiously. 'Are you all right? You look very pale.'

'I didn't sleep very well,' I admitted.

'Eat something,' she advised, but every mouthful I took felt like cardboard.

'I saw a poster for the fair over in Trewissick,' Mum said. 'This afternoon—we should go. It's got some big rides.'

'Oh, *yes*,' Imogen and Joe chorused enthusiastically.

Mum smiled. 'I didn't know you were into rides, Imogen.'

Imogen nodded. 'I wasn't, but now I am. The bigger the better!'

Mum glanced at me. 'Hopefully you'll feel better later, Holly. Why don't the three of you find something quiet to do this morning?'

Imogen shot me a look and then said, 'That's a good idea. We could stay here and read. I've got my sketchbook.'

Mum nodded. 'Excellent idea. I've got plans but I'll only be out for a couple of hours. We could take the car over to Trewissick for lunch and then go on to the fair; what do you think?'

'Sounds great,' said Joe.

While Mum brushed her teeth, Imogen leaned over to me. 'That's worked out well, hasn't it?' she asked cheerfully in a low voice. 'It gives you time to go down the mine this morning and . . . *you know* . . .' She mimed, **BOOM**!

I bit my lip. 'Yeah. Boom. Right.'

'Don't worry, I'll come with you,' she added brightly.

'*No!*' I said, horrified. With no sense of danger, Imogen would be a liability in the mine.

Her face fell. 'I was just offering. Because I know you don't like it down there.'

'Thanks,' I said. 'That's really kind of you, but I'll be OK. Maverick will be there.'

'He is *so* cool,' Imogen sighed, and her face went all kind of dreamy. 'Do you think he'd let me have a go on his motorbike?'

'No,' I said shortly. 'He's in enough trouble over the tranquillizer as it is.'

'The what?'

'The thing he used on the beach. Oh, you won't remember.'

'Do you think he gets into trouble a lot?' Imogen asked.

I hesitated. Was that why Steve had assigned him to us? To get Mav off his back? 'I don't know.'

'Wonder what the most dangerous thing is that he's done,' mused Imogen, a light in her eyes. 'I'll ask him.'

'You're not coming,' I told her. 'You have to stay here. It's not safe.'

She sulked. 'You're such a spoilsport.'

How I wished I had the antidote right there and then to turn Imogen back into the friend I knew!

'You can help me,' Joe told her. 'I'm designing a bomb.'

I was horrified. 'A *bomb*?! Joe, are you totally insane?!'

He looked offended. 'It's not insane. We need to protect ourselves against Macavity. This would be lightweight and portable. Like a grenade. But I'm not very good at drawing.'

'I can draw!' exclaimed Imogen.

He nodded. 'If you can do the diagrams, I can make the prototype. It's really easy to get hold of explosive materials if you know how.'

I couldn't believe what I was hearing. 'Joe, you could get into SO much trouble. You can be locked up for making a bomb!' I put my head in my hands. 'How can I go out now? I'll come back to find you've blown yourselves up experimenting!'

'Honestly, sis, I'm not an idiot,' Joe said crossly. 'I'm supposed to be your *mentor*.'

'Not while you're infected with the venom,' I told him sharply. 'I can't trust a word you say. You've gone bonkers—both of you.'

Imogen took my hand and squeezed it. 'Holly, I'm still me. I know we've been stung, but honestly, it doesn't feel that scary. Whatever this stuff is, I just feel more *alive* than ever. Like I want to do everything, try everything, because we only get one life, don't we?'

I blinked tears away. 'I don't want you to die.'

She laughed. 'You are funny. I don't want to die either! I want to *live*!'

Mum came out of the little bathroom, and I wiped my eyes quickly so she wouldn't see. 'Right,' she said. 'I'm off out—got my mobile if you need me. I'm grabbing a couple of things in town and then meeting up with Mike. So if you can't get me, Julie will be able to get him. Stay here, okay? Holly, you need to rest. Play a board game or something.' She smiled. 'See you in a little while.'

I tried to stretch my mouth into a smile.

The door closed. 'Right then,' I said, and *almost* managed to keep my voice sounding normal. 'I'd better go.'

Imogen gave me a big hug. 'Knock 'em dead,' she said, which didn't make me feel any better.

Joe did a fist bump. 'Make sure there's nothing left of the little critters,' he said in a terrible American accent.

'Please,' I said. 'Please don't do anything crazy. Not until I get back, all right?'

They both gave me a thumbs-up, which didn't reassure me in the slightest. 'Don't worry about us. Everything's going to be fine!'

I took a deep breath. The sooner I got there, the sooner I'd be back.

I opened the door, made sure Mum was no longer in sight, and started off. Towards, if not certain death, then certain terror. Which was almost as bad.

CHAPTER 21

The gate to the mine was padlocked, but I simply climbed over it and into the silent grounds. The tall chimney and the crumbling buildings felt eerie even in the bright sunshine of the day. There was no sign of Maverick, though a big black car was parked to one side of the building. Was that him? I headed over, but the car was empty.

I waited a bit longer, checking my watch. It was just after nine o'clock. Tours started here at ten, so I didn't have all that long to get down and do what I needed to do. Would Mav have gone down into the mine without me? He'd just said 'see you there'. Maybe 'there' meant down in the tunnel?

I shifted from foot to foot in an agony of indecision. I hadn't wanted to come, but now that I was here, I just wanted to get it over with as quickly as possible. I couldn't afford to wait any longer. Hopefully the car was Mav's and he was already in the mine, waiting for me. If he wasn't . . . well, I would have to get on and do my job, wouldn't I? It wasn't like I didn't know what to do. And every minute I was away from Imogen and Joe increased the likelihood they'd do something stupid.

The thought galvanized me into action. I ran to the lift shaft. Grabbing a hard hat and a head torch from the crate, I yanked open the metal doors of the lift and jumped inside. A thick cable hung down from the wall with two buttons—one for down, one for up. I pressed the 'down' button, scrabbling to get my hat on at the same time.

Nothing happened. I pressed the 'up' button. Nothing.

Did they switch the electricity off in this place when they weren't using it? Or had the lift broken? But then how would Maverick have got down?

I didn't have time for all this . . .

I had forgotten just how deep the mine shaft was. It felt like FOR EVER before I reached the bottom.

There was no Maverick. Where was he? Had he decided I didn't need any help after all?

There's no point asking yourself stupid questions, I told myself sternly. You're on your own, Electrigirl. Get on and get out.

Which tunnel was it? There were two!

I chose the one on the right, and headed along, trying not to think about ANYTHING AT ALL, especially not the TONS OF ROCK above my head that would kill me instantly if they fell down.

And THEN up ahead, I heard a sound. Someone was talking. I hurried towards it. Mav!

But as the voice grew louder my steps faltered, and all the hairs on my neck stood up.

It wasn't Mav.

It was another voice I knew well.

A voice that had no expression in it at all. And even though I couldn't make out the words, even though it was still only a murmur carrying through the dark, dusty air of the tunnel, I knew it instantly.

It was HER voice.

CHAPTER 22

Professor Macavity. The person I was most frightened of in the whole world. She was here, in the mine! I stopped, gasping, reaching for the walls to steady myself. My head whirled. Was Mav down here too? Had she kidnapped him? Was he—oh no—was he *working* for her all along? Was I walking into a trap?

The voice murmured on, low and insistent. I knew I had no choice. I was down here now and if I ran away . . . well, who would destroy the piskies then? I had to go on. I'd known that one day we'd meet again. Her message had promised it:

I KNOW WHO YOU ARE AND WHAT YOU ARE.

I DON'T FORGET MY ENEMIES.

ONE DAY, YOU AND I WILL MEET AGAIN, ELECTRIC GIRL

It was Macavity who had given me my superhero name. It was thanks to the CyberSky mobile phone mast that I had powers in the first place: the lightning streaking across the sky that day had crashed into it and then blasted me unconscious. I still didn't know how or why.

But here she was. And this time, I wasn't imagining it.

I switched off the head torch as I crept

closer. I didn't want to be discovered until the last possible minute. I made as little noise as possible as I reached the shaft open to the sky— the one that had the opening to the narrow, angled tunnel where the piskies were hidden. Macavity's voice echoed from that tunnel. She was in there, with the piskies.

I stepped in and began to creep forward.

The professor's voice was louder now, clearer. '. . . weren't ready yet. And now the whole project has had to be brought forward because some of them swarmed too early . . .'

I felt a grim satisfaction that I had already destroyed a large number of the piskies.

'. . . No, the government cleared up. At least, I assume so. We can't wait now. The risk of discovery is too great. Send them out today— otherwise the whole experiment is wasted.'

Another voice spoke—a man's. But not, to my enormous relief, Maverick's. It said, 'What about the girl? Has she been infected?'

'Not as far as we can tell,' Macavity said in that grey monotone that sent shivers down my spine. 'It does not matter. It's an unfortunate coincidence that she happened to be here. My intel failed to warn me—the officer concerned has been . . . dealt with. But Holly Sparkes won't get in my way a second time.'

I gasped, and then clapped a hand over my own mouth, furious with myself for making a noise. All those times the others told me I was crazy to imagine that Macavity was obsessed with bringing me down—here was the proof!

'She's just a girl,' the other voice suggested.

Macavity snapped back, 'She is *not* just a girl! She's an extraordinary creation.' Her voice slowed. 'It's a shame she isn't working for me. I have wondered whether she might be persuadable, given the right circumstances . . .'

Never! I wanted to shout. I would never work for you! You're a dangerous evil lunatic! I pressed a hand to my mouth to stop myself making a noise.

'We could wait until the fuss has died down,' the other voice said.

'No!' Macavity was sharp again. 'I need a proper demonstration. Something big, to show how people can be goaded into mass action. The venom is strong, but the human sense of self-preservation is hard to overcome. I need to show that it only takes one person to lead the way—and then the rest will follow, like sheep.

Or lemmings. You jump, I jump, as the saying goes.' An amused tone had crept into her voice.

The man hesitated before saying, 'It's a lot of people to use in a demonstration.'

The professor made a noise of contempt. 'It's necessary. Then I can sell this invention to the highest bidder. Imagine how many governments will be interested! Imagine how many dictators could take control of their countries if their population is self-destructing! The value is immeasurable.'

'I'm sure you've set a price,' said the other voice, dryly.

There was a low bubbling noise that I'd heard only once before, and it had made my blood run cold then, too.

She was laughing.

And that made me take the final steps into the cave, out of the tiny tunnel, sparks tingling around my fingers. The two figures standing in the cave, surrounded by walls of glittering piskie wings, turned in surprise.

'Hello, Professor Macavity,' I said.

'WE MEET AGAIN.'

CHAPTER 23

As opening lines went, it wasn't very original, I admit. But it felt right to say it. And the effect on the professor was immediate. Her eyes narrowed to grey slits, and her hands tensed into fists. I imagined those square-cut nails digging into her palms. She looked exactly as I remembered her: grey suit, grey hair cut into that straight bob, grey shoes. Angles and edges; nothing soft about her at all.

'Holly Sparkes,' she said, and there was almost an inflection of surprise in her voice. 'Or should I say *Electrigirl*?'

I shrugged. 'Either will do.' Yeah, I was thinking, I can do this. Joe would tell me to stand up to her. That's what I'm going to do! 'Call off the experiment,' I said. The man standing just behind her was short, with a thick beard. He held an electronic tablet and looked most alarmed to see me.

The professor did not look alarmed. Instead, her eyebrows rose into triangular points. 'I don't think so.'

'People are going to die,' I told her. 'Do you really want their blood on your hands?'

She did that eerie bubbling laugh again. 'Have you been taking lessons in superhero language? Or are you naturally over-dramatic?'

My face went red. 'If people die because of the piskies, it'll be your fault.'

'Piskies?' Now she was properly laughing. Her mouth opened wide as the horrible sound came out. 'I never thought anyone would seriously believe that. My experiment has been more successful than I imagined.' The laughing stopped. The eyes narrowed. 'And I can imagine a *lot*, Holly Sparkes.'

'Yeah?' I said. 'So can I. I can imagine you in a prison somewhere. With—with dripping walls, and no toilet. And no window.' I suddenly realized I was describing some kind of dungeon, or possibly Azkaban. British prisons probably weren't like that.

'Your imagination never was your strong point,' said the professor. 'How is your clever friend, by the way?'

'Her name is Imogen,' I said, feeling anger rising. 'And she's absolutely fine, no thanks to you and your piskie minions.'

Professor Macavity's eyes gleamed. 'She's been *stung*? Interesting. I'd be fascinated to study the effect on her brain, given the changes I worked on it through the mobile phone—'

I was furious. 'She is NOT some kind of body you can just experiment on!'

The professor smiled. 'Everyone is an experiment. Even you, Electrigirl.' She gave a quick sigh. 'I really don't have time to chat. Goodbye, Miss Sparkes. There's nothing you can do now. In only seconds, you'll know *exactly* what it's like to have that lust for danger . . . and then you won't be my problem anymore.'

As she turned and headed to the furthest corner of the cave, the man with the beard tapped on the tablet. Instantly, hundreds of eyes gleamed green in the darkness. And I heard the sound of thousands of synthetic wings unfurling.

Oh no, I thought. No you don't. Not while I'M here . . .

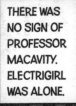

THERE WAS NO SIGN OF PROFESSOR MACAVITY. ELECTRIGIRL WAS ALONE.

Oh no!

I will NOT be buried alive down here!

I took great gulping breaths. There was a distant rumble under my feet, and a plume of dust rose from the shaft behind me. I'd made it out! My heart was racing faster than I'd ever known it, and my lungs felt like they were full of dust, but I was out! And the piskies were destroyed!

For a moment, I felt triumphant. And then panic gripped me. Where was the professor? Was she lying in wait for me somewhere? I whipped around, trying to look in all directions at the same time, but there was no sign of her. This exit had brought me out in an unfamiliar place and for a moment, I wasn't sure where I was. And then I caught sight of the main building about a hundred metres away, surrounded by its crumbling partners. My breath coming in ugly gasps, I set off towards it. I couldn't let Macavity slip through my fingers. All the time she was free, I would always be looking over my shoulder. I had to find her while I still had the chance.

But when I reached the buildings, the big black car was gone. The gate was now open, the padlock hanging clear. There was no sign at all of Macavity. In fact, there was no sign of anyone at all. I glanced at my watch. It was after 10 a.m. Shouldn't people be here for the tour? I needed to warn Mike that the tunnel had collapsed! I also needed to find Mav— where was he? Why hadn't he come? *And* I was desperate to get after Macavity somehow!

I said some very rude words to myself. What should I do now? The best option was probably to head back to the caravan site. I could find Julie there, and get a message to Mike about the mine. And I could also check on Joe and Imogen. Were they still safe? My feet started to run of their own accord. Every thudding step seemed to increase the panic in my chest, and I sprinted the final four hundred yards to the caravan park.

The little Portakabin by the site gate was empty and I said another rude word to myself. No Julie, no Mike. Where WAS everyone today?! I ran on to number seventeen, relieved to see that it was still standing unscathed. But even before I reached the door, I could see the note stuck to it. 'Oh no, oh no,' I panted. Where were they? What had they done?

I had run out of rude words. They were up on the cliffs! How long would it be before the urge to do something dangerous grew too strong? Everything else flew out of my head. I had to get to them before it was too late.

I whirled to set off towards the sea and crashed into another person, knocking us both to the ground.

'Oof!'

'Cameron!' I scrambled off him. 'What are you doing here? I'm sorry, I have to go—my brother—'

'I have to go too!' he said, beaming. 'I came to tell you—I have a mission!'

'You have—what?'

He flexed his muscles. 'I am Invinciboy! People need my help!'

'What—what are you talking about?'

'The mine! It's collapsing! Mum got a call just a few minutes ago—there's a tour party trapped down there. She's on her way there right now—and I'm going to save my dad!' He turned to run.

'NO!' I yelled. 'You mustn't go!' Thoughts whirled around my head. I'd got everything in the wrong order! I should have called the police or something before I came here—the tour party must have already been in the lift shaft when I left. They'd been on their way down when I'd caused the rock collapse! I felt faint with horror. 'The emergency services,' I said to Cameron. 'Has someone called them?'

Cameron laughed. 'Of course! But they don't know the mines like I do. I'm going to save the day! Aren't you coming?

'I can't,' I said, feeling sick. 'I have to find Imogen and Joe. And Maverick. Everyone's in danger. I can't be everywhere at once.'

Cameron shrugged. 'Suit yourself. I'd have thought you'd *want* to come. Seeing as your mum's down there too!'

CHAPTER 24

For a second, everything went black, and my knees buckled.

Mum—in the mine. *That* was her plan for the morning, to go down the mine? Had she said? Had I not been listening?

'It's all right.' Cameron was starting off. 'I can handle it. Leave this to me.'

'No.' I grabbed his arm to stop him going. 'No—you mustn't.'

'They need a superhero,' he said simply.

And suddenly, strength flooded through me. 'Then there's one right here,' I said, straightening up. 'It's my job.' Can't be everywhere, huh? I'd show her! I was ELECTRIGIRL!

Cameron pouted. 'I want to do it. I never have any fun.'

'I have a job for you,' I said, my mind racing. I faced him seriously. 'I have something very important for you to do—a mission. Are you sure you're up to it?'

He practically grew ten centimetres. 'I'm sure! What do I have to do?'

'Imogen and Joe have gone to the cliffs,' I told him. 'They went for a walk, but I've thought of something much more exciting we could do. And—er—dangerous.'

Cameron's eyes lit up. 'What do you have in mind?'

'Trenarth Peak,' I said. 'It's got a really steep rock face. You said you wanted to go climbing—well, only experienced climbers are supposed to go up there.'

'That's right!' Cameron smacked a fist into his other hand. 'They always say it's too dangerous for kids. Brilliant idea!'

'Go and find Imogen and Joe,' I told him, 'and say I'll meet you all at Trenarth.' Trenarth was a bus ride away. This would at least buy me some more time.

Cameron nodded, grinning. 'So you're going to get the people out of the mine, right? You will make sure my dad's okay, won't you?'

I was relieved to see that the venom hadn't made Cameron completely unfeeling. 'Of course I will,' I said reassuringly, hoping I could deliver.

He high-fived me and set off towards the coast, yelling back, 'See you there!'

'Oh!' I called back, a new idea striking me. 'Get Joe to call Maverick and ask him if he wants to come too, okay?' At least that way *someone* would try to make contact with Mav!

'Okay!' he yelled.

I took a breath and turned to face the park exit—the path I'd thudded down only minutes earlier. Time to go back.

Back to the collapsed mine, and the darkness.

The darkness that I'd hoped never to go into again.

But there were people trapped down there.

Not just people. My mum.

WOULD i BE iN TiME?

CHAPTER 25

As I ran towards the mine, I could feel my powers building. If people were trapped under tons of rock, I'd need everything I could muster to rescue them. How did you rescue people trapped in mines, anyway?

A siren blared, and I jumped onto the grassy verge to avoid the fire engine racing past. If the firefighters were on their way to the mine, and if they'd been stung . . . would that make them better at their job or worse?!

As I dashed through the open gates, I could see people standing around, their faces worried, some of them with mobile phones clamped to their ears. Cameron's mum, Julie, was there, too—I was amazed that so many people had appeared in such a short time.

The fire engine was parked alongside one of the ruined buildings, its single wall jutting up into the sky. Two firefighters talked quietly together by the cab. I sidled closer, trying to hear.

'. . . five of them,' the first one said. He was tall and handsome, with a determined expression.

'They're actually still in the lift?' asked the second. She was shorter than the man but looked strong and fit. Her blonde hair was tied back in a ponytail.

'Yeah,' he said. 'Lucky they hadn't yet got out of it. The collapse happened just as they reached the bottom, apparently. That's what Mike told me on the radio. He's the one leading the tour. Good thing they were still in the lift, or we'd have no way of communicating. There's an alarm in it, goes straight to the emergency services.'

'So they're protected by the cage,' the woman said, nodding. 'That was very lucky.'

'They're all uninjured,' the man said. 'But Mike says they can't see a thing and they're covered in dust. The whole lift is buried under rocks.' He lowered his voice. 'Which means the air supply is limited.'

The woman paused. 'How long have they got?'

He shrugged. 'You know it's impossible to say. Another hour, maybe?'

'An hour . . .' She turned and looked at the mine shaft. 'But we need contractors with lifting equipment . . . specialists . . . It's not enough time.'

The man caught sight of me, and his face changed. 'Hello, love, you all right?'

'My mum's down there,' I said, and swallowed. 'Are you going to get her out?'

He smiled reassuringly. 'Course we are. We have to take it slow, though. Can't risk any injury.'

I swallowed again. 'But . . . the air . . .'

He pressed his lips together for a moment and looked at me seriously. 'How old are you, love?'

'Twelve.'

'Well, I'm not going to lie to you. It's a tricky one. We have to get the rocks off the cage before we can lift it—and there may not be much time. We're working on a plan. There's a guy with rock-lifting equipment on his way.' He gave me a nod and turned back to his colleague. Four more firefighters were gathering at the back of the engine. The woman reached into the cab for the radio.

I glanced around and took a few steps away from them. Over by the main building I could see Julie, her face streaked with dust and tears, talking to other worried-looking people. There were people everywhere—too many. How could I do anything without everyone seeing?

I couldn't help it.

MY POWERS, ALWAYS ACTIVATED BY A FOCUSED, INTENSE FEELING, SPRANG TO MY FINGERTIPS . . .

CHAPTER 26

The people coming out of the cage all looked identical: covered in grey dust, choking and spluttering. The firefighters were pulling them away from the mine shaft as quickly as they could, offering them water and making them sit down at a safe distance.

An ambulance squealed in through the gates, lights flashing, siren wailing.

But where was my MUM?

I gazed desperately at the grey people. One . . . two . . . three—there was Mike, Julie rushing to clasp him in her arms as he stumbled to the ground—four . . .

Five people went down, the firefighters said. Five. Where was the fifth?

And then a shout went up from near the cage. 'Paramedic!' and my heart almost stopped.

A body was being pulled out from the rubble.

Grey hair tumbled over the grey face. A streak of blood ran down one cheek.

My mum.

My knees gave way from under me, and I sank unsteadily to the ground. My fingers still tingled from the after-effects of the electricity, but my powers had faded again. Had I done that? Had breaking up the rocks caused one of them to hit my mum? Had she breathed in too much of the dust I had created?

Was she dead?

They put her on the ground, and a paramedic brought over some kind of machine with a face mask. I guess they fitted it to her face but there were too many people in the way. All I could see was her feet. I stared at them, willing them to move.

Come on, Mum . . . Come *on* . . .

And then they twitched, convulsively, and even from here I could hear the awful coughing and retching sounds, but it didn't matter how bad it sounded because she was **ALIVE**.

My whole body started to shake.

Someone put a blanket around my shoulders. 'All right there?' It was the female firefighter. She sat down and smiled at me. 'Your mum's going to be OK, I'm sure. She just inhaled a lot of dust.

They'll take her to hospital—you can go too, I'm sure. Looks like I'm going to need a lift back to the station myself, seeing as our engine was just totalled.' She smiled at me again. 'What a day, eh?'

I tried to smile back, but my mouth was all wobbly. 'Yeah.'

'I'm Halina,' she said. 'What's your name?'

'Holly,' I said automatically.

'Well, Holly,' said Halina, 'are you OK? Jaz and I got a really big electric shock back there when we touched you. Didn't you feel it?'

I felt my eyes open wide in alarm. Deep inside me, something went **WARNING, WARNING!!** And I could practically hear Joe's voice shouting, *'DON'T TELL HER ANYTHING!'*

Joe! And Imogen! Had Cameron persuaded them off the cliffs? Were they on their way to Trenarth to try rock climbing?

'She's going to be OK, you said?' I slipped off the blanket and got to my feet.

She got up too. 'Yes, but—'

'I've got to go. Please look after her.'

I could hear her calling after me as I ran, but I didn't look back. Mum was *alive*, that was the important thing.

Joe and Imogen might not be.

CHAPTER 27

The sun was high in the sky as I ran down the road, trying to muster every bit of strength I had left. I wasn't even sure which way I should go. The bus to Trenarth Peak left from the middle of town, but if they were still on the Polcarrow cliffs, I would waste valuable time running in the wrong direction!

Reasoning that I should check the nearest place first, I ran on towards the coast. A mile passed, then two. It was ominously quiet as my feet thudded on the tarmac. Where was everyone? It was the height of summer; there should be people walking along the roads, cars, kids flying kites . . .

As the coastal path led me up to the cliffs, I knew why. They were all there. Everyone. Hundreds of people, gathered in a huge flock on top of the dark grey rocks, which rose out of the hillside like emerging giants. They were so close to the edge—too close. I'd grown up with coastal paths. Back home in Bluehaven, my favourite place was on a hilltop overlooking the sea. But the ground at the edge wasn't safe—everyone knew that. Cliffs crumbled into the sea; if you stood on the wrong part, the earth would just slip silently from under you, and there you were, smashed on the rocks below.

I slowed to a jog, my heart thumping from the run but also from fear. There were a LOT of people. What were they all doing here? I looked about frantically. I couldn't see Cameron—or Imogen, or Joe.

And then I heard a voice. A cold, grey voice, strangely at odds with the bright sunshine, amplified so that it boomed out across the hillside.

And my feet, having brought me to the very edge of the crowd, suddenly refused to take another step.

'Good afternoon!' the voice said. 'It's wonderful to see so many of you here today. Who's ready for the thrill of their lives?'

I felt like I'd run into a brick wall. It was wrong, all wrong. The voice was Macavity's, but the words sounded like something from a TV gameshow. It made my head spin. What was she talking about?

There was an answering murmur from somewhere near the front of the crowd.

'I said,' Macavity repeated in her monotone, 'who's ready for the thrill of their lives?'

This time the response was louder. I felt sick. This must be her great 'demonstration'—but what kind of thrill was she talking about, up here on the cliffs?

Her words from the mine thudded into my head like tombstones:

You jump, I jump, as the saying goes . . .

She was going to make everyone jump off the cliffs! *That* was the demonstration of the power of the venom! But jumping from here was insanity! The blue water below the horseshoe-shaped rocks was far too shallow!

'There's no health and safety form here,' Macavity went on, 'just a pure adrenalin ride, from the top of the cliffs to the splash pool below. And don't forget to smile for the cameras!'

Instinctively, I glanced around. Standing here and there, taller than head height, were grey metal towers, topped with speakers and video cameras, their lights blinking red. We were all being recorded!

I didn't have much time. Whatever I was going to do, I needed to do it fast. I started pushing my way through the crowd. There was every type of person here: old people, small children, surfers, people in business suits, parents with shorts and sunburn. I saw sting marks on lots of them, though others were trying to hold them back.

'Don't,' one girl begged her boyfriend. 'Please don't—it's too dangerous.'

He laughed. 'Come on, where's your sense of adventure? I've always wanted to do something like this!' But he held back, I noticed. There was a flicker of doubt in his eyes.

I felt a tiny glimmer of hope. It took a lot to make people risk their lives. The venom couldn't overcome *all* human reflexes then. People weren't just jumping blindly into the water. Many of them were local; they knew perfectly well that the sea wasn't deep enough here. Jumping from this height risked serious injury, if not death. But what had the professor said? *It only takes one person to lead the way—and then the rest will follow . . .*

'Who's first?' asked the professor calmly. 'Who's got the guts to take the first step?'

I doubled my efforts to get through the crowd, pushing and shoving. 'Excuse me, can you just—coming through, sorry . . .'

I heard someone say enthusiastically, 'Soon as I see the first one do it, I'm in there!'

If I could reach the professor before anyone answered her challenge, maybe I'd have a chance to stop this . . .

'We have a volunteer!' Macavity's voice rang out, and her usual monotone wavered in excitement. 'Speak into the microphone, young man. What's your name?'

'Joe,' said my brother.

I FELT ENERGY SURGE THROUGH ME.

CHAPTER 28

Joe and I were airlifted out of the water, which was pretty cool. By which I mean, of course, utterly terrifying. Once we were hauled into the helicopter, Steve gave me a right telling-off about knocking out so many people.

'What else could I have done?' I shouted over the noise of the rotors. 'They were about to jump off the cliff!'

'So you thought you'd electrocute them all instead,' Steve shouted back sarcastically. 'Perfectly safe.'

'It seemed like the better option,' I said, glaring at him. 'How did you get here so fast, anyway? I thought you were in Scotland.'

'I was. Came down this morning. It's possible that the Scotland job is connected to Macavity.'

I stared. 'What? How?'

He shook his head. 'Classified information,

sorry. But my lab finally finished working on the antidote, so I was on my way here anyway.'

'The antidote?' I felt immensely relieved. 'You mean, you can turn everyone back to normal?'

Joe groaned. 'It's no fun being normal—OW!' He glared at the woman withdrawing a needle from his arm.

The woman who'd picked up the piskies from the beach—Lin—stared impassively back.

'Oh, it's you,' I said, feeling my face heat up in embarrassment.

She gave me a nod and the hint of a smile, slid the syringe back into a canister and then disappeared into the cockpit.

'Lin's our co-pilot,' Steve said.

OMG. She could fly a *helicopter* too? 'Whoaaaa,' I said, awed. Cameron wanted to be Maverick? I wanted to be *Lin*!

Joe swayed. 'My head feels . . . gloopy.'

'Have you tested this?' I asked Steve, putting my arm around my brother.

He nodded. 'Yep. Just now. On him.' Then he saw my face. 'Of course we've tested it! And it contains just a little sedative to make the last hour seem like a dream.'

'You're going to be okay,' I told Joe, hoping

I was right. 'What about Professor Macavity?'

'There's a team on the ground right now,' Steve said. 'We're nearly there.'

We landed at a safe distance from the rocks, and as soon as the door slid back, I ran towards them, ignoring my dripping hair and clothes. Not too far off, I could see a handful of people in black clothing, packs on their backs and monitoring devices in their hands. They were going from person to person on the rocks, checking pulses and pulling tiny syringes from their backpacks which they jabbed swiftly into arms and legs as they went.

'Mav!' I shouted, seeing someone I recognized.

He turned and grinned when he saw me. 'Hey, kid. Sorry about this morning. I was called into the office at short notice to be told off.'

'For what?'

'Taking the tranq without asking.' He rolled his eyes. 'Honestly, it's like they want to keep all their toys to themselves! I called but no one answered your phone. I hoped you wouldn't go into the mine without me, but I guess you couldn't wait to destroy the robots, huh?'

'I thought you were down there!' I exclaimed. 'I spent half the time thinking you'd been kidnapped!'

He let out a huge laugh. 'Brilliant. Well, I can tell you, Electrigirl, if I *were* kidnapped, I'd definitely count on you to rescue me.' He waved an arm across the sea of people, many of whom, to my great relief, were sitting up and blinking. 'You did an awesome job here. To knock out this many people and not kill them? That takes skill, girl. You saved their lives. You deserve a medal.'

I blushed again, feeling so much better about it all suddenly. 'Oh, I don't know about that.'

'You knocked those out at the same time,' Mav said, nodding towards one of the grey towers. The camera on the top was smoking gently, its lens cracked right across. 'Honestly, Holly, I don't think anyone could have done a better job.'

Imogen came weaving towards me, her eyes unfocused. 'Holly? Is that you?'

'Yes! Yes, it's me! Oh, Imogen!' We shared a shaky hug. 'Are you okay? I'm so sorry I knocked you out!'

'Is that what happened?' Imogen rubbed her neck. 'I have no idea. What were we all doing up here anyway?'

I explained. She looked appalled. 'I remember . . . everything seeming so exciting. And like nothing bad could happen to me. Even jumping off the cliff seemed like a really cool thing to do. I was just waiting for someone else to go first—and then I'd have followed them.' She shuddered. 'That stuff! It might have killed us all!'

'Don't worry,' I told her. 'Steve's brought the antidote. That's why you're not crazy anymore.'

Cameron joined us. 'Antidote? Antidote to what? Is that what all these people are doing with hypodermic syringes? Has it been properly tested? You can't just go around injecting people!'

I grinned. 'Welcome back, Cameron.'

Joe came up behind me. 'We're going to have a hard time explaining this to Mum.'

The world whirled. I staggered. 'Mum! How could I have forgotten?! We have to get to the hospital!'

'What? Why?' Joe stared at me, eyes wide. 'What's happened to Mum, Holly?'

'She—down the mine! There was a rockfall! I . . .' I trailed off.

Cameron suddenly said, 'My dad! He was down there too! Was he—did you get him out?'

'I got them all out,' I said, my hands starting

to shake. 'Your dad's fine—at least, he looked like it. It was just Mum! She—we have to go—now!'

'Steady.' Mav caught us up. 'Your mum's fine. Bump on the head and broke her wrist. Cameron, your parents are at the hospital too, but they're fine. We'll get you all over there.' He signalled, and Lin came over.

'Can you get the kids to the hospital?' he asked her.

She nodded. 'They've already OK'd us to land on their helipad.'

Cameron went pale. 'We're going in a *helicopter*? Do you know how dangerous those things are? They crash *way* more than planes.'

Lin fixed him with a steely glare. 'I think you'll find my safety record is immaculate.'

Cameron dropped his gaze. 'Oh,' he mumbled. 'Okay.'

I sighed. Could Lin BE any more awesome?

'You go,' Mav told me. 'We'll clear up here.'

'We certainly will,' Steve agreed. 'Mav's on clearing-up duty for the next month.'

As the four of us and Lin headed back to the helicopter, I could hear Mav complaining, 'How many times! I was only *borrowing* it . . . !'

Within minutes, Joe, Imogen, Cameron, and I were flown (after Cameron insisted that Lin did the safety checks three times) to the hospital where we met up with Mum, and Cameron's parents. There may have been some crying. And it wasn't all me.

Mum had her arm plastered in the afternoon, and then we ate a huge meal in the hospital canteen because traumatic events make you very hungry.

As we were sitting in the cafe, I caught sight of Steve through the window and made an excuse to leave the table.

'We've dosed everyone now, we think,' he told me. 'It took a while, but we've got them all. And a team has been assigned to the mine, to seal it off from the public and spend time checking it for rogue robots.' Then he hesitated. 'There was a bit of a problem on the cliffs, though.'

'A problem?' I asked. 'What sort of problem?'

He gave an exasperated sigh. 'We lost her. The professor.'

'You *what?*!'

'I don't know how. The person assigned to guard her looked the other way for a moment— and she was gone. We're searching. She can't have got far.'

I didn't believe *that* for a minute. I felt slightly sick. 'She's back out there again, free?'

'I'm afraid so. But listen—we've got eyes everywhere. We'll find her.'

'Before she finds me?' I snapped. 'Like last time?'

'I know, I know. I'm sorry about that. I'm detailing two extra agents to your case. It looks like the Scotland thing might be developing, but I can't be sure yet. It might all tie up together, which makes it all the more exasperating that we've lost her. I'll know more in a few days. In the meantime, your mum can't drive because of that broken wrist.'

'I know.' I glanced back through the window. Mum was listening intently to Joe but her eyes were fixed on me. It made me feel a little nervous. Was she suspicious? She mustn't know about my superpowers. They had to be a secret!

'So one of my agents will also be your driver for the week.'

'Huh? You mean, like a chauffeur?' I was WELL impressed.

'Yep. I figure the department can stand the expense. And I need him out of my hair for a while anyway. The lad drives me nuts.'

'Who?' I asked, though I'd already guessed.

Maverick came up, beaming. 'Hey!' he said. 'I've got a caravan next to yours. Just shout if you need me to take you anywhere. I'm going to soak up some rays.' He caught Steve's eye. 'Er. I mean, I've got some paperwork to catch up on.'

I felt better already. 'That's so cool,' I said. 'You can keep an eye out for Macavity, too. Save me looking over my shoulder all the time.'

He snapped his fingers. 'Gotcha. Don't you worry, I won't let her go a second time!'

'A second time?' I said, puzzled.

His face froze, comically. 'Ah. Steve didn't tell you? I mean . . . er . . .'

'You were the one who was supposed to be guarding her?' I said.

'Look, there was a lot going on . . .'

'I'm sure you're going to have a wonderful week,' Steve said with a thin smile.

Mum, Imogen, and Joe came out of the doors. 'Hello,' Mum said to Steve, offering her unhurt hand to shake. 'I don't think we've met.'

'Steve Sloane,' he said, shaking her hand gently. 'I work for the security services.'

Mum tilted her head to one side. 'Which ones?'

He smiled blandly. 'The good ones.'

'My husband's in the army,' she said. 'I hear all kinds of things. How do you know my daughter?'

I held my breath. What would Steve say?

The truth, of course. Or part of it, anyway. 'We met in Bluehaven,' he said, 'after the accident at the CyberSky building.'

Mum's expression cleared. 'Ahh! I see. That explains it. You were the people who cleared it all up.'

'That's right.'

'Was it a security issue, then?'

Steve smiled blandly again. 'I'm afraid I can't possibly comment on that, Mrs Sparkes. I was very sorry to hear about your accident here.'

She looked ruefully down. 'Yes. So inconvenient.'

'My department would be very happy to help out,' Steve said. 'Since your accident is part of a wider investigation. I'm assigning a driver to you until your wrist is healed. In fact,' he shot a sidelong glance at Maverick, 'feel free to use him for any personal errands you need running, or to clean the oven or anything else.'

Mum, who had been about to protest, hesitated. 'Oh. Well . . . hello.'

'Hello.' Maverick reached out to shake her hand. 'Maverick. Good to meet you.'

'*Maverick*?' she repeated. 'Really?'

'Um . . .' Maverick shuffled his feet and suddenly looked about six years old. 'No, it's a nickname.'

'What's your real name?' Mum asked.

'Er . . . Asif.'

'Well, Asif, it's a pleasure to have you along. You can keep an eye on the kids, since they can't seem to help getting into trouble.'

'That's not true!' I said indignantly.

Joe was enthusiastic. 'Mav's going to stay with us! Awesome!'

'Next caravan along,' I said.

From round the side of the building Cameron appeared with his parents. 'Holly!' he said, waving. 'Isn't it great that everyone is all right?'

Mike, Cameron's dad, was frowning down at his phone. 'The collapse of the mine is all over the news already,' he said. 'We're going to lose revenue.'

'I'm sure we can arrange compensation,' Steve said smoothly.

Mike looked at him in surprise. 'Who are you?'

'Government,' said Steve. He glanced at his watch. 'Time to go. Keep in touch, Mav.' He nodded briefly at me and then went.

Mike held out his phone to us. 'Look at this! I can't work out if this is a spoof article.' He grinned. 'Superheroes in Polcarrow!'

A wave of fear washed over me. 'Can I see?' asked Joe, sounding almost normal.

He, Imogen, and I crowded together to read . . .

POLCARROW BUGLE

SUPERGIRL SAVES HOLIDAYMAKERS

Reports are coming in of a fantastical event up

on the Polcarrow cliffs earlier this morning. With no clear reason why, a large party of tourists gathered to try tombstoning—which, as any *Bugle* reader knows, is too dangerous to attempt on this part of the coastline—but a collective attempt to jump was foiled by a freak event, caused, it appears, by a schoolgirl.

'She just came out of nowhere,' said Shelley Trott, aged 30. 'This girl. Blasting light from her hands. I was too far off to be hit by it, but I saw them all go down, like a pack of dominoes.'

Neil Haigh, aged 23, had a slightly different take on events. 'It was a shockwave,' he said. 'I've felt one before. I'm in the navy. I don't know how it happened or where it came from, but it wasn't anything to do with a girl. No human can make a shockwave like that. You need a powerful generator. Trust me.'

Sidney Hiller, aged 73, disagreed with them both. 'It was a bolt from above,' he said. 'God knew we were all at risk. I don't even know why I went down there. My wife Carole wanted me to come. I hate the water. I can't swim. But God was watching over us. He sent a miracle. I'll be giving extra thanks from now on.'

Mandie Preston, aged 40, summed it up. 'I don't know what happened. Everything's a bit fuzzy. But I do know one thing. Today has been a very odd day indeed. And now I'm going home for a cup of tea and a sit down.'

I let out a breath. So close to discovery . . . !

'Time for a costume,' Joe muttered in my ear.

I sighed. 'All right, you win. But no tights. No *way*.'

Imogen whispered. 'I could design you something. I think it's a good idea.'

'All right.'

I handed the phone back to Mike. 'Weird,' I said. 'Glad it's over now, though.'

'No more weirdness,' Mum said firmly, pulling me into a one-armed hug. 'This is meant to be a *holiday*!'

We trooped out to the car park. It was a beautifully warm evening, and I couldn't believe so much had happened in just one day.

'We could have supper on the beach,' Joe said.

'You've just eaten a huge meal!' I pointed out.

'So? I've got a lot of catching up to do.'

Mike laughed. 'Kids, eh? All the same.'

'I'm not,' said Cameron, offended.

Mike laughed and ruffled his hair. Cameron looked appalled at this.

'Don't worry, Cameron,' Joe said, 'we know you're different.'

'That's why you're our friend,' added Imogen. 'Different is cool.'

Cameron gave a wide smile. 'You're my friends, too. And tomorrow I'll show you my secret place. One no one knows about.' His parents crossed to their car.

'You haven't captured a mermaid or anything, have you?' I teased.

'Of course not. Everyone knows mermaids don't exist.'

'Neither do piskies,' muttered Joe. Mav gave him a playful punch on the shoulder.

'Piskies, eh!' he said. 'You kids and your imaginations!'

Mum laughed with him. 'People are funny, aren't they? According to one of the firefighters, you were at the mine this morning, Holly. And the firefighter said that as soon as I was brought to the surface you ran off! I told her it couldn't be you. My daughter wouldn't run off knowing I was injured, I said.'

'Er,' I said.

'But then Julie came to see me,' Mum went on, her tone sharpening. I looked around, frantic for an escape. 'And she said she saw you there too, but she didn't see when you disappeared. And now I find out you were on top of a cliff, far too near the edge, I suspect, and caught up in some kind of bizarre stunt. Not only that, but you seem to have got yourself involved with a government agency. Your father will *not* be impressed.'

'Um . . .' I said.

Mum waited for a moment, but when it was clear I wasn't going to say anything else, she said, 'When we get back, I'm going to make a cup of tea. And then, Holly Sparkes, we're going to sit down together, and you're going to tell me **EXACTLY** what's been going on.'

I'd faced two enormous crises today. But this was WAY bigger.

How on earth was I going to deal with this one?

As Mum got into the passenger seat of the car, Imogen and Joe edged closer to me. 'Don't worry,' Imogen whispered. 'We'll figure it out.'

'Your secret identity will be safe,' my brother added.

I grinned. Evil geniuses, curious mums . . .

ABOUT THE AUTHOR

Jo Cotterill believes that superheroes are really important. They are what we can all aspire to be: people who use their powers to fight evil and help others. When she's not trying to change the world, Jo makes up stories in her very untidy office-come-craft room, sometimes stopping to write music instead. Her other books include the *Sweet Hearts* series for Random House and the critically-acclaimed *Looking at the Stars*, which was nominated for the Carnegie Medal. Jo lives in Oxfordshire with her husband, daughters and two over-indulged guinea pigs.

jocotterill.com

ABOUT THE ILLUSTRATOR

Cathy Brett has been a theatre scenic artist, school art technician, college lecturer, fashion illustrator, packaging designer, jet-setting spotter of global trends and style consultant to the British high street. These days she loves drawing more than anything else. Ever. Except her nieces. And cake. Drawing her nieces while eating cake would be utter bliss.

Cathy lives and works in a shed/studio at the bottom of a Surrey garden.

cathybrett.blogspot.co.uk

CREATE A SWARM OF FLYING PISKIES...
USING THE POWER OF ELECTRICITY!

YOU WILL NEED:

- Balloon
- Tissue paper
- Pencil
- Scissors
- Sticky tape
- Your hair (If you haven't got any hair, a woolly jumper will do)

template

1. Place the tissue paper over the template of the piskie and trace it with a pencil. Then cut it out. Repeat until you have several piskies. Spread them out on the floor.

2. Blow up the balloon and tie the neck in a firm knot (an adult may be helpful here, since balloon-tying can be fiddly).

3. Rub the balloon rapidly on your hair for at least ten seconds.

4. Now move the balloon slowly through the air a little way above the tissue piskies. They should leap off the ground and cling to the balloon, just like the swarm in the cave!

HOW DOES IT WORK?

When you rub the balloon against your hair, the surface of the balloon collects invisible 'electrons' which carry tiny amounts of negative electrical charge. Positive charges are attracted to them, which is why something very light (such as tissue paper) will be pulled towards the surface of the balloon.

Ready for more great stories? Try one of these...

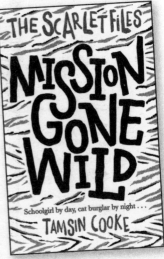